Nicholas Gilroy

Viva Christo Rey

Father Stephen Gemme
Deacon George O'Connor

Chapter 1
Meeting Raphael

Nicholas always enjoyed riding the bike he received as a birthday gift from his grandmother when he was twelve-years old. Returning to Saint Peter's High School Seminary with it was a momentary stroke of brilliance. *It must have come from Our Lady,* he thought. Now that he had his bike with him at school and Jose was bringing his, they would be able to bike around Baltimore together.

Both sides of Roland Avenue, the smooth, winding road that Nicholas was navigating, had quaint shops and single-family homes. After what felt like a long summer, he was excited and happy that he was returning for his second year at the seminary. Nicholas was pumping so hard his bike began to move faster and faster.

Baltimore was always warm in August and September. Today, the first day of September, was no exception. Even though the momentum of the moving bike created a breeze that swept over him, sweat from the heat of the bright sunshine was running down his forehead.

So much had happened to him during his first year at Saint Peter's. He thought about all the friends he had made and all the new experiences, especially becoming the star kicker for the football team. He thought about Brendan and the other homeless men who were given shelter and help at Saint Peter's.

Overcome with a sense of sadness, Nicholas's thoughts lingered on the terrible violence he had encountered when he volunteered to help tutor children in the inner city. His sadness suddenly disappeared, and he felt at peace when he began to think about helping Theresa in math and reading and of his special friendship with her brother, Adam.

He was filled with gratitude as he reflected on the wonderful teachers at Saint Peter's, especially their kind and gentle rector, Father David Kelly. His thoughts then focused on the strict, but fair, vice rector, Father Stephen Reynolds, who had shown him amazing compassion and care when he so greatly needed it.

As the vice rector, Father Reynolds had high expectations of all the boys enrolled in the seminary. Nicholas's initial fear of this priest was transformed into admiration, and now he did not want to let Father

Reynolds down. With the help of Our Lady he was confident he would be able to do his best his sophomore year.

And football! The season was on and practice would begin right away. As an upper classman, Nicholas knew he would have more responsibility, especially in helping the incoming freshmen. There had been talk of making him the co-captain of the team, but it was only talk. He realized that his ability to kick a football came from God, so he prayed for humility and for gratitude that God would bless him and his teammates with another good season.

Nicholas felt in his heart that God was at work in all these experiences, even if he didn't always understand how and why. Having a strong faith in God helped him through the many challenges that he faced his first year at Saint Peter's High School Seminary, and he knew this same faith in God would also help him one day as a Catholic priest.

"Hail Mary, full of grace, the Lord is with thee…," prayed Nicholas as he pedaled his bike. His mother had taught him to always ask Our Lady for help and guidance, especially when he was participating in activities such as riding his bike. She told him that prayer would keep him focused on God and lead him to virtue.

His prayers suddenly came to a halt when a delivery truck pulled out in front of him. Although Nicholas immediately slammed on the brakes, his bike skidded out of control underneath him.

Overcome with fear and helplessness, Nicholas turned his head and closed his eyes, praying out loud, "Dear Lord! Please help me!"

Suddenly, he was airborne. He felt himself being lifted up and when he opened his eyes, he saw what looked like the wings of an angel. The weight of his bike and backpack were gone as Nicholas flew over the delivery truck, landing on the other side.

Breathing heavily and feeling light-headed, he heard the man in the truck shout at him to be more careful as he pulled away, even though it was clear that the truck driver was at fault.

Before he could process what had happened, Nicholas was surprised to see a man standing next to him. He was about the same height as Nicholas, which made him seem small for a grown man, and he was dressed like one of the seminary's gardeners. His tan face was framed by short, curly brown hair. However, it was this man's eyes that made a big impression on Nicholas. They were dark brown, and the pupils in the center of each eye seemed to be illuminated by a light that made them twinkle.

"Amigo," the man said gently. "That was a close call. But I can see you have powerful friends," gesturing to the Miraculous Medal that Nicholas was wearing. His mother had given him the medal when he made his First Holy Communion.

"Anyone who is close to Our Lady has powerful friends because when Our Lady comes to us many angels come with her. I think, my friend, that one of her angels must have carried you over that truck."

"Yes, he sure did," Nicholas panted, clearly out of breath from his brush with death.

A sense of curiosity overcame Nicholas as he asked, "Sir, who are you?"

Smiling, the stranger responded, "My name is Raphael. I am one of the gardeners at Saint Peter's. And haven't I seen you there?"

"Yes, I am a sophomore, and my name is Nicholas Gilroy."

"Oh yes, the famous football kicker! I have heard much about you this summer from the other staff. You helped all those men that were homeless."

Nicholas thought, *how could he know about that*? "I was one of the guys that helped. It really was a group effort."

"Any time we help those who are lost, or alone, or afraid, we help the Master, Himself," Raphael said with great reverence. "Matthew 25. Yes?"

"Yes, exactly."

There was something remarkable about this humble man that made Nicholas feel as though he was in the presence of a holy spirit. He felt inspired and safe with this stranger who he had just met.

"Well Amigo, it was nice to meet you and I know I will see you again. Oh, there is your friend, Jose."

How did he know Jose's name? Nicholas thought, as he watched Jose approaching fast on his bike, waving and smiling. But when Nicholas turned back to Raphael, he had disappeared into thin air.

"Hey, buddy!" Jose exclaimed, dismounting his bike to give Nicholas a big hug. "Good to see you!"

"Yeah, me too."

More shaken by the sudden disappearance of Raphael than his near-death experience of almost crashing into a truck, Nicholas cried out, "Did you see where Raphael went?"

"Who is Raphael? I didn't see anyone."

Jose's answer was what Nicholas needed to affirm that he had truly experienced something miraculous.

Slowly measuring every word he spoke, Nicholas replied, "Raphael was standing right next to me. He said that he is one of the garden workers at Saint Peter's, and I think he saved my life from crashing into a truck. And there is something else . . . I almost don't want to say."

Jose now grew anxious for his friend and asked, "What is it?"

Smiling, Nicholas replied, "I think he might be an angel."

Chapter 2
Roommates

Nicholas and Jose walked slowly in silence toward the massive front oak panel doors of Saint Peter's. Looking up at the castle-like structure, which now felt like his second home, Nicholas remembered a prayer for students by Saint Thomas Aquinas:

Come, Holy Spirit, Divine Creator, true source of light and fountain of wisdom! Pour forth your brilliance upon my dense intellect, dissipate the darkness which covers me, that of sin and of ignorance. Grant me a penetrating mind to understand, a retentive memory, method and ease in learning, the lucidity to comprehend, and abundant grace in expressing myself. Guide the beginning of my work, direct its progress, and bring it to successful completion. This I ask through Jesus Christ, true God and true man, living and reigning with You and the Father and Holy Spirit, forever and ever. Amen.

The importance of prayer was always with Nicholas whenever he was working or playing his favorite sports of football and soccer. Seeking to know and love and serve God was important to him and was always in his heart.

It was Jose who broke the silence. "Wow, it's good to be back. So different now that we are sophomores. I have to confess that a year ago, I didn't know what to expect and I was a little nervous and afraid."

"You, nervous and afraid," Nicholas said, laughing. "How do you think I felt. You at least went to a public school with other kids. I was homeschooled by my mom and dad and I only had my sister, Elizabeth, as a classmate. The thought of going to a public school terrified me."

"Well, God must have had a plan because you have me as your new roommate."

"Yes, when I received the packet from Saint Peter's, I was so happy to see that we were going to be roommates." With a big grin, Nicholas continued, "Besides, God wants me to keep you out of trouble."

"Okay, I won't get in trouble, if you make sure that you don't snore. I need my beauty sleep at night."

Nicholas said frowning, "I don't snore . . . not too much. Come on let's find our room."

Excited with the possibility that as a sophomore one of his missions would be to help the new freshmen adjust to life in the seminary, Nicholas entered the building. The boys encountered many of their classmates, and ringing back and forth were calls of "hi guys" and "welcome back."

Their summer vacation over, the returning seminarians were filled with energy, since the beginning of the school year was a time of much activity. All the boys were happy to see their friends and classmates again. Throughout Saint Peter's High School Seminary, the atmosphere was filled with the joy, grace and love of God.

The freshmen and sophomore dorm rooms were on the third floor, which was called the Saint Francis Wing. Nicholas was extremely happy to discover that, as in his freshman year, his new room was on the same side of the seminary's inner courtyard. As he looked out of the big window, he could see the beautiful, tall, marble statue of Our Lady of Mount Carmel holding the infant Jesus surrounded by four small water fountains with small marble angels. One of the seminary's gardeners was taking care of the many beautiful flowers that were planted between the water fountains. Straining to see if it might be

Raphael, Nicholas was very disappointed when he realized that it wasn't.

Each dorm room was designed for two boys to live together. It had two twin beds, two small desks with chairs, two small bureaus, and one closet. For drinking, washing and brushing teeth, there was a white porcelain sink, and over the sink was a mirror for grooming.

There was one thing that distinguished the rooms on the Saint Francis Wing from the other rooms in the seminary. Every room had a beautiful San Damiano Crucifix on the wall. Painted on this icon cross was the image of Christ along with the images of saints and people that had some connection with Christ's crucifixion.

In the 12th century when Saint Francis of Assisi was in his early twenties, he was praying alone in front of a crucifix in an abandoned chapel in San Damiano. Suddenly, Francis heard these words of Christ: "Francis, repair my house, which is falling into ruin."

Francis at first thought that Christ wanted him to rebuild the abandoned chapel. It was only later that he realized Christ was asking him to rebuild the spiritual life of the Church by bearing witness to the saving power of the Gospels.

Nicholas and Jose couldn't wait any longer to be part of the laughter and activity that was coming from the hallway.

"Come on, let's find Luke's room," Nicholas exclaimed, referring to Luke Perkins, his roommate his first year. Nicholas continued, "I wonder who his roommate is?"

"Hopefully, they get along. In fact, I hope we get along," mused Jose. "Just remember that I am the room boss and what I say goes." Jose then tossed the pillow on his bed and hit Nicholas.

"Oh, I don't think so." Nicholas grabbed his nearby soccer ball and threw it at Jose.

Always quick to respond, Jose dodged the ball and it bounced off the wall and out into the hallway.

Nicholas shouted, "Nice job, Jose!" He tumbled out into the hallway after the ball and bumped into Father Reynolds.

The vice rector was a mountain of a man, muscular and disciplined. His hair was cut short, like that of a Marine drill sergeant, and he was dressed in a jet-black cassock, perfectly pressed. He had a prayerful aura about him that communicated an unspoken respect.

With blue eyes that were piercing and sharp, Father Reynolds said in a playful tone, "I see that you are ready for soccer season, Mr. Gilroy."

"Sorry, Father, my aim was a little off. I was hoping to hit Jose."

Father Reynolds turned his attention to Jose. "Mr. Romero, are you provoking your new roommate? A bit early in the semester for that, don't you think?"

"No, Father, I was only setting up the rules for the room. Mr. Gilroy needs to remember the virtue of obedience!"

"As do we all," the priest acknowledged.

He then asked, "How was your summer vacation?"

"I had a wonderful summer vacation." Jose continued, "I went with my mom and dad and brothers and sisters to Ponce in Puerto Rico to visit by grandmother. She is so happy that I am studying to be a Catholic priest. She prays the Rosary every day for me and for all the seminarians here at Saint Peter's."

Now it was Nicholas's turn to respond. "I didn't travel as far as Jose, but my mom, dad, sister Elizabeth, and I spent a week with my grandmother, who lives in Connecticut. She lives in Mystic, so we had a great time visiting the seaport and going to the ocean. My grandmother also prays the Rosary every day; and when we were with her, we all prayed together. I also played a little soccer this summer and it was fun. Although I think I will always love football."

"Both of you boys are blessed to have grandmothers who are women of faith. It is important for all of us to pray Our Lady's Rosary each day."

Looking right at Nicholas, Father Reynolds continued, "Mr. Gilroy, your knowledge of soccer may come in handy someday. Now don't forget to retrieve the soccer ball that went bouncing down the hall, and God bless you both."

"Thank you, Father," the boys said in unison.

As soon as Father Reynolds turned to go, Nicholas jogged after his soccer ball. Tossing it to Jose, he exclaimed, "What do you think he meant by soccer coming in handy someday?"

"Only God knows for sure," Jose responded with a laugh.

Chapter 3
The New Seminarian

"It had to be you guys making all that racket. It looks like you wanted to make sure everyone knew you were back." Standing in the doorway of the room next to Nicholas and Jose was their good friend from freshman year, Luke Perkins. "And what was all that commotion about?" Luke asked.

"Oh, that was only Nicholas turning the hallway into a soccer field." Jose, who was more demonstrative than Nicholas, gave Luke a bear hug and exclaimed, "Wow, what happened? It looks like you've grown a foot."

"Yah, I did grow, but it was only two inches. It had to be all that healthy Wisconsin air, along with my job at a local lake as a lifeguard teaching young kids how to swim. All that swimming stretched my body."

Nicholas, laughing, greeted his old roommate with a hug that was less intense and shorter than Jose's. "I bet it was hard for Saint Peter's to find you a roommate better than me."

Now it was Luke who was laughing as he responded, "As a matter of fact, I bet they did have to search all over Saint Peter's for your replacement. They did come up with a good one. Remember Alan Nowicki. Well, we're practically neighbors. He comes from Duluth, Minnesota, and I can understand him. He says, 'a can of pop', not 'a can of soda' like you guys."

Jose quipped, "When in Rome, my friend!"

Nicholas, so happy to be reunited with both of his friends, piped up, "Instead of holding up the wall in the hallway, Luke, why don't you come inside and see our room."

Once in the dorm room and with the door closed, the boys could really cut loose with much chatter and laughter as they recounted their summer vacations. The noise in the room was so loud that no one heard the knocking on the door at first. But it wasn't long before Nicholas realized that someone was outside.

Opening the door, Nicholas was so surprised that he was speechless.

"Hey, man. I bet you didn't expect me!" Standing in front of him was Adam Marshall, an African-American, teen-age boy with the biggest grin on his face and with big brown eyes flashing in anticipation.

Overcome with emotion, Nicholas immediately gave Adam a big hug and exclaimed, "Wow! It really is you, Adam, and you really are here at Saint Peter's."

"I'm not only at Saint Peter's, I'm two doors down in room 333, just like the nine choirs of angels."

Nodding his head in agreement, Nicholas said, "Adam, this has to be a sign from God that He wants you here because that was my room last year, and I, too, thought of the nine choirs of angels."

Now it was Jose and Luke's turn to greet Adam as they gently pulled him into the room. The boys were eager to hear why Adam Marshall, tough guy and former gang member, was at Saint Peter's studying to be a Catholic priest like them.

Turning to Nicholas, Adam said, "Nicholas, when I came to see you the end of the school year, I wanted to thank you for helping save my sister's life. You didn't care about your life, only Theresa's life. It took courage to grab her away from Kane."

"Adam, you're the one that saved Theresa. God gave me the courage to help you, that's all," replied Nicholas, full of humility.

Adam continued. "But what was even more important, I had to tell you about my miraculous experience with Our Lady. Nicholas, remember when we first met. Even though you were pretty scared of me, you didn't back down. In my heart, I knew that you had something that I didn't have."

Pausing, Adam then said, "In my sadness because of what happened to Lemont, I turned to Mary, the great Mother of God. That is when she spoke to my heart and told me that she would always be with me to protect and guide me to her Son. Nicholas, then I understood your love for her because I, too, fell in love with her.

"Something was happening to me. I had this overwhelming desire to pray, especially to pray Our Lady's Rosary. The more I prayed to Our Lady, the more I knew that I didn't want to continue with the life I was leading as a gang member. I also realized that I needed to go to Confession to be free of my past.

"Somehow, I was changing. I was growing closer to Our Lady, and she was bringing me closer to her Son. Then one day when I was praying after receiving Holy Communion, I heard in my heart Jesus Christ say, *will you follow Me?* And without hesitation I said, '*Yes,*' and I was filled with a peace and a love that I have never known before."

In a tone full of gratitude, Adam continued. "Because of you, Nicholas, I had already met Father Reynolds, so I turned to him. He gave me the guidance and support that I needed. Like a Marine drill sergeant, he made me work like I was in boot camp. All summer long he had me reading books on our Catholic faith and reading books on the saints.

"To discern if Saint Peter's was where God wanted me to be and to have the courage to do the Will of God, Father Reynolds also guided me spiritually. I began praying Our Lady's Rosary every day and began attending daily Mass as much as I could and reading the bible. Father Reynolds was so good to me. Once a week, I would come to the chapel and he would expose the Blessed Sacrament so that I could spend an hour with Our Lord in adoration.

"At the same time, because I had skipped school so much, my grades had to improve to even think of taking the entrance exam at Saint Peter's."

"I know who helped you. Your grandmother!" Nicholas cried out with great joy.

"Yes, my grandmother would spend hours every day helping me with my subjects. And, of course, Theresa was always trying to encourage me by telling me that she was praying that I would be just like her friend, Nicholas, and that I would be going to Saint Peter's to be a Catholic priest.

"Well, I did pass the entrance exam. Although I will have to stay back a year and begin as a freshman. God certainly had a plan when He put you and I together, Nicholas. I feel that God wants me to be a priest. But really, can I do it?"

Without hesitation, Nicholas said, "Of course, you can do it, Adam. You have great qualities. You are brave and strong and you have experienced many things most of the guys here at Saint Peter's have only seen on TV or in a movie. Your life experiences will help you someday be a more compassionate and understanding priest."

"I'm glad you think so." As he rested his hand on Nicholas's shoulder Adam in a voice full of compassion said, "Thank you, my friend."

Nicholas, so very thankful to Our Lady for Adam's conversion and for leading Adam to her Son, Jesus Christ, silently prayed: *Oh, Blessed Mother help Adam and help me be obedient to the Will of God so that we will be able to serve Him some day as Catholic priests.*

Chapter 4
Class with Father Reynolds

Nicholas was eagerly anticipating the first class of his sophomore year with Father Reynolds. *Wow, this is way different from last year,* thought Nicholas, while remembering how he felt intimidated by the commanding presence of the vice rector. But appearances can be deceiving. Over the course of his freshman year, Nicholas had learned a lot more about the person named Father Stephen Reynolds. Because of the compassion and wisdom of this priest, Nicholas was given the help and spiritual guidance he so greatly needed during one of the most difficult times of his life.

Yes, Father Reynolds has been an awesome spiritual father to me, Nicholas thought.

As soon as Father Reynolds entered the room, the boys spontaneously sat upright with all eyes focused on their teacher. Because he had high expectations for all the young men in his class, he took the training of these seminarians for the priesthood very seriously. He knew that for a young man to become a priest, he would have to have a love for the Sacraments of the Catholic Church.

The rows of desks were kept neat and straight, and there was no talking unless one was called upon. Turning to the clean white board, Father Reynolds wrote, *Article 2: The Paschal Mystery in the Church's Sacraments.* All the seminarians typed what was on the board onto their smartbook computers.

"Gentlemen, open up your Catechism to page 293." Now scanning the class, Father Reynolds said. "Mr. Romero begin reading Number 1131."

In a strong voice Jose began. "Number 1131. The sacraments are efficacious signs of grace, instituted by Christ and entrusted to the Church, by which divine life is dispensed to us. The visible rites by which the sacraments are celebrated signify and make present the graces proper to each sacrament. They bear fruit in those who receive them with the required dispositions.

"Number 1132. The Church celebrates the sacraments as a priestly community structured by the baptismal priesthood and the priesthood of ordained ministers.

"Number 1133. The Holy Spirit prepares the faithful for the sacraments by the Word of God and the faith which welcomes that word in well-disposed hearts. Thus, the sacraments strengthen faith and express it.

"Number 1134. The fruit of sacramental life is both personal and ecclesial. For every one of the faithful, on the one hand, this fruit is life for God in Christ Jesus; for the Church, on the other hand, it is an increase in charity and in her mission of witness."

As soon as Jose had finished reading, Father Reynolds said, "Gentlemen, it is the priesthood of ordained ministers that you are being prepared for here at Saint Peter's. Like me, as future priests, you will preside at the sacraments. It is a sacred and holy responsibility. You will be charged with the defense of the sacraments and to properly prepare the people of God to receive them."

Turning to the white board again, Father Reynolds wrote: *Article 1: The Sacrament of Baptism.* Again, all the seminarians typed what was on the board.

"Mr. Gilroy, on page 312 begin reading Number 1213."

In a clear voice, Nicholas began. "Number 1213. Holy Baptism is the basis of the whole Christian life, the gateway to life in the Spirit (vitae spiritualis ianua) and the door which gives access to the other sacraments. Through Baptism we are freed from sin and reborn as sons of God; we become members of Christ, are incorporated into the Church and made sharers in her mission: Baptism is the sacrament of regeneration through water in the word.

"Number 1214. This sacrament is called *Baptism*, after the central rite by which it is carried out: to baptize (Greek *baptizein*) means to 'plunge' or 'immerse'; the 'plunge' into the water symbolizes the catechumen's burial into Christ's death, from which he rises up by resurrection with him as 'a new creature'.

"Number 1215. This sacrament is also called '*the washing of regeneration and renewal by the Holy Spirit*,' for it signifies and actually brings about the birth of water and the Spirit without which no one can enter the kingdom of God.

"Number 1216. This bath is called *enlightenment*, because those who receive this (catechetical) instruction are enlightened in their understanding . . . Having received in Baptism the Word, '*the true light that enlightens every man,'* the person baptized has been *'enlightened,'* he becomes a *'son of light,'* indeed, he becomes *'light'* himself."

"Thank you, Mr. Gilroy. Gentlemen, it is through the Sacrament of Baptism that we receive the Holy Spirit and become members of the People of God and of the Body of Christ, which is the Church. By Baptism, God purifies us from sin.

"Baptism is the sacrament of faith which has the Risen Christ as its source, and it is the offer of salvation for all people. Linked intimately to Confirmation and to the Eucharist, Baptism is, with these two sacraments, Christian initiation."

Opening his Catechism Father Reynolds began to read, "Number 1272. Incorporated into Christ by Baptism, the person baptized is configured to Christ. No sin can erase this mark, even if sin prevents Baptism from bearing the fruits of salvation. Given once for all, Baptism cannot be repeated.

"Number 1273. Incorporated into the Church by Baptism, the faithful have received the sacramental character that consecrates them for Christian religious worship. The baptismal seal enables and commits Christians to serve God by a vital participation in the holy liturgy of the Church and to exercise their baptismal priesthood by the witness of holy lives and practical charity.

"Number 1274. The Holy Spirit has marked us with the seal of the Lord (Dominicus character) for the day of redemption. Baptism indeed is the seal of eternal life. The faithful Christian who has 'kept the seal' until the end, remaining faithful to the demands of his Baptism, will be able to depart this life marked with the sign of faith, with his baptismal faith, in expectation of the blessed vision of God—the consummation of faith—and in the hope of resurrection."

Pausing, Father Reynolds asked, "What is the matter and form of Baptism?"

Looking at the many raised hands, Father Reynolds called out, "Mr. Romero."

"The matter is the water and the form are the words of baptism, *I baptize you in the name of the Father and of the Son and of the Holy Spirit.*"

"Yes, spot on!"

Father Reynolds addressed Nicholas, whose hand was still raised. "Yes, Mr. Gilroy?"

"Father, is it true that priests and deacons can preside at a Baptism?"

"The ordinary ministers of Baptism are the priests and the deacons, and even the bishop." After pausing for a dramatic effect, Father Reynolds continued. "In the case of an emergency, like a person who is in danger of dying because of illness or an accident, then anyone can baptize, even a person who is not baptized can baptize."

There was a gasp of surprise from the class and then Father Reynolds asked this question, "How can this be possible? Well, all that is required is the right intention and the trinitarian formula and water. This is the first sacrament and one must be baptized to receive the other sacraments. Also, the trinitarian formula, *I baptize you in the name of the Father and of the Son and of the Holy Spirit* is essential for a valid baptism."

Now Father Reynolds began reading from the General Instruction. "By Baptism we are freed from the power of darkness and joined to Christ's death, burial and resurrection. We receive the Spirit of Filial adoption and are part of the entire people of God in the celebration of the memorial of the Lord's death and resurrection.

"Baptism incorporates us into Christ and forms us into God's people. This first sacrament pardons all our sins, rescues us from the power of darkness, and brings us to the dignity of adopted children, a new creation through water and the Holy Spirit. Hence, we are called and we are indeed the children of God."

With his hand raised, Luke asked, "Father, if Baptism takes away sin, why do we still need to go and take part in the Sacrament of Reconciliation each month here at Saint Peter's?"

"Excellent question, Mr. Perkins. If you have been reading the Catechism, perhaps you have come across the word concupiscence. What is concupiscence?"

The class was silent. Nicholas had heard the word, but he was not sure of the definition.

"Gentlemen, concupiscence is understood as an effect of original sin that remains after Baptism. The waters of Baptism cleanse us of original sin itself, but concupiscence remains as a lingering effect. Number 1264 in the Catechism of the Catholic Church teaches that certain temporal consequences of sin remain in the baptized, such as suffering, illness, death, as well as an inclination to sin that Tradition calls concupiscence.

"We have free will, and we can sin, and we do sin. So, we need to go to Confession on a regular basis. But that tendency for sin does not take away any of the wonder or joy of Baptism."

Finished with the lesson, Father Reynolds handed out a paper titled *Renunciation of Sin and Profession of Faith* to each of the seminarians.

"Gentlemen, after every question reply *I do.*"

"Do you reject Satan?"

All the seminarians responded, "I do."

"And all his works?"

"I do."

"And all his empty promises?"

"I do."

"Do you believe in God the Father, almighty, creator of heaven and earth?"

"I do."

"Do you believe in Jesus Christ, His only Son, Our Lord, who was born of the Virgin Mary, was crucified, died, and was buried, rose from the dead and is now seated at the right hand of the Father?"

"I do."

"Do you believe in the Holy Spirit, the Holy Catholic Church, the communion of saints, the forgiveness of sins, the Resurrection of the body and life everlasting?"

"I do."

"This is our faith. This is the faith of the Church. We are proud to profess it, in Christ Jesus, Our Lord."

"Amen," the seminarians responded.

"It is essential that this be said at every Baptism." Then Father Reynolds asked this question, "At what Mass is this said during the liturgical year?"

"Easter!" replied the class.

"Very good, gentlemen! I want you to read the rest of the chapter on Baptism in your Catechism. Class dismissed."

Chapter 5
The Retreat

It didn't take Nicholas long to get back into the routine of seminary life. Relishing all the new knowledge that he was learning in his sophomore classes made him more fully alive. He especially was thankful for daily Mass and the time spent in prayer and in Eucharistic Adoration because it gave him a sense of peace and it inspired him to follow Christ as a Catholic priest.

The words of Saint Augustine of Hippo, "*You have made us for Yourself, O Lord, and our hearts are restless until they rest in You,*" would come to him often, and it was affirmation that he was on the path that God wanted him to be on.

In the Gospels, many times, Jesus would go away by Himself to pray. From the earliest days of the Church, men and women followed the example of Jesus. This great tradition of growing in the spiritual life is called a retreat.

Taking the time to rest, pray, reflect, and do penance is deeply important for every human being.

We are created in the image and likeness of God, and a retreat gives us the time and the opportunity to grow in our relationship with Him. To be human, we must seek to grow in holiness and charity. It is through retreats that we are given the opportunity to do this. Retreats also help us grow in obedience to the God who created us and loves us.

It was Friday and the first week of school at Saint Peter's had come to an end. Dinner was a joyous occasion with laughter and chatter among the seminarians. All the young men were full of excitement as they made their way to the grand hall for their first three-day retreat of the school year.

Dressed in their house cassocks, they gathered in the grand hall dedicated to Saint John Vianney, patron saint of parish priests. The grand hall was as old as the seminary itself. It was designed to accommodate the 140 students enrolled at Saint Peter's.

A giant mural of the Last Supper by the Renaissance artist, Vicente Juan Masip, adorned the front wall of the hall. The main purpose of this magnificent picture was to draw the minds of these young men to the glory of God. Studying the images, Nicholas wondered where he might have been seated if he had been living at that time. Then he realized that every time he attended the Holy Sacrifice of the Mass, he was present with Our Lord at the Last Supper.

Smiling as he watched the seminarians enter the grand hall, Father Kelly thought, *What fine young men.* Rector of Saint Peter's High School Seminary, he was a gentle soul. The kind of priest you would want to go to if you faced a dilemma or crisis in your life. His desire to grow in holiness and charity was evident in his manner and in his words.

As soon as all the seminarians were seated, Father Kelly began, "In the Name of the Father and of the Son and of the Holy Spirit. Loving and merciful God, we ask for Your help and guidance as we begin this new school year with our annual retreat. We ask our patron, Saint Peter, to pray for us, that we can grow in wisdom. We ask Our Blessed Mother Mary to pray for us, that we can grow in patience. Above all, let these days of reflection, penance, and prayer lead us to You, so that we may discern Your Holy Will for us and gain the courage to be obedient to Your Will. We ask all this through Jesus Christ, Your Son, who lives and reigns with You and the Holy Spirit, one God forever and ever. Amen."

Father Kelly stepped aside and the vice rector took his place at the lectern. The strong and imposing figure of Father Reynolds seemed more serious than ever.

Scanning the assembled seminarians with his sharp and piercing eyes, the vice rector asked, "Gentlemen, would you give up your life for Jesus Christ? As future priests and disciples of Jesus, each one of us is called to give our life for Christ. In the Gospel of Matthew, Chapter 16, Jesus says, '*Whoever wishes to come after me must deny himself, take up his cross and follow me. For whoever wishes to save his life will lose it, but whoever loses his life for my sake will find it. What profit would there be for one to gain the whole world and forfeit his life? Or what can one give in exchange for his life?*'

"As men of prayer, each day we are called to ask Our Blessed Lord to help us grow closer to Him. These three days of retreat are an opportunity for each of us to live this passage from Matthew's Gospel.

"In the history of the Church, thousands have come forward and sacrificed their lives to defend our faith. In the 1920s in Mexico, President Plutarco Elías Calles and his government began persecuting the

Catholic people. At first, he took the property of the churches. All Catholic churches, schools and institutions were closed and the Catholics of Mexico were forbidden to practice their faith. But his hatred for the Church had no limits and he then began to kill priests and burned the churches down.

"Known as the Cristero War, the Mexican people were forced to react, and an army of fifty thousand Catholic soldiers took up arms against the government to defend their faith. These soldiers were called Cristeros because every time they charged into battle they would shout, *'Viva Christo Rey! Long live Christ the King!'*

"In 1927, when Mexico was immersed in this violent religious persecution, there was a young man, Jose Sanchez del Rio who was fifteen-years old. Since he was a child, he had a great love for Jesus in the Blessed Sacrament. He was always encouraging his friends to have more devotion to Our Lord and Our Lady of Guadalupe.

"Every time Jose heard about the glorious battles of the Cristeros, which his two older brothers were fighting in, his desire to join the holy army would grow stronger. Finally, Jose wrote a letter to General

Prudencio Mendoza pleading to be allowed to fight. Because he was so insistent, General Mendoza gave Jose a special assignment, to be the flag bearer for the Cristeros.

"Jose quickly earned the nickname, Tarcisius, because of his zeal for standing for Jesus Christ and the teachings of our Catholic faith against an oppressive government seeking to destroy the Church.

"Now Saint Tarcisius was a young man who lived during the Christian persecutions in the third century in Rome. One day when he was taking the Holy Eucharist to the condemned Christians in prison, he was attacked and beaten to death. Saint Tarcisius gave his life to defend Our Lord in the Holy Eucharist from the desecration of the pagans.

"It was on January 25, 1928 that Jose showed his courage and love of Jesus. During heavy fighting, the horse that General Mendoza was riding was suddenly killed. Jose caught sight of the General on foot and he knew that the General was extremely vulnerable. Without any thought for himself, Jose gave the General his horse so that the fight for religious freedom could go on. Seeking cover, Jose began firing at the enemy until he ran out of ammunition. He was then captured by the government's soldiers.

"Jose was locked up in the sacristy of a church that had been turned into a prison. However, also with him were expensive fighting roosters that one of the guards had placed for safe-keeping. Jose was so upset that God's sacristy was being used as a barnyard that he caught all the prized roosters and snapped their necks. It wasn't long after this that the enemies of Christ the King decided to kill him.

"On February 6, Jose wrote a letter to his mother telling her that he was a prisoner and that he would die soon, but that he would die happy because he was going to die for God. '*Send my regards to everyone one last time and finally receive the heart of your son who loves you so much and wanted to see you before dying.*'

"Jose remembered what his mother had taught him. He prayed the Rosary of Our Lady of Guadalupe, asking for comfort and strength.

"In an attempt to break his spirit, Jose witnessed the execution of a Cristero soldier. Before the soldier was killed, Jose encouraged the man by telling him not to be afraid, for soon they would both be in heaven with Jesus and Our Lady of Guadalupe.

"On February 10, 1928, Jose was forced to walk to his execution. His torturers had cut off the soles of his feet and struck him savagely with sharp machetes. With every blow Jose would cry out, *'Viva Cristo Rey.'*

"The soldiers offered to spare his life if he said, *'Death to Christ the King.'*

"Jose's only response was, *'Long live Christ the King! Long live Our Lady of Guadalupe!'*

"Since the road was nothing but rocks and dirt, the stones where Jose had to walk were soaked with his blood. When he got to the cemetery he was bleeding heavily; and although he screamed in pain, he did not give in. Finally, Jose was stabbed and shot. Before his final breath, he made the sign of the cross in the sand with his blood.

"Saint Jose Sanchez del Rio stands for us today as a modern-day martyr for our Catholic faith. Where did this young man find his courage? He drew his strength from Our Blessed Lord in the Eucharist. He drew his strength from Our Blessed Mother in the Rosary. He drew his strength from the great gift of faith given to him by God.

"Saint Jose Sanchez del Rio knew in his heart that Christ is our King and Lord, and that our lives should give glory to Him every day. Gentlemen, during these days of retreat, ask Saint Jose to pray for you and, when you pray your Rosary, think of his sacrifice for the Church asking God to give you the courage to act when needed and to be steadfast in your faith, no matter what difficulties you may face in life. Amen."

Chapter 6
Mass with The Cardinal

Nicholas had enjoyed attending and taking part in the Holy Sacrifice of the Mass from a very early age. He especially liked all the Masses celebrated at Saint Peter's. The priests made sure that the music and the Mass flowed together for a near-perfect praise of Almighty God.

The first retreat of the year at Saint Peter's was coming to an end. The weekend for the seminarians had been filled with peaceful and powerful moments of prayer. The praying of the Rosary, the exposition and benediction of the Blessed Sacrament and the singing of the "Salve Regina" were beautiful, spiritual devotions that lifted the minds and souls of the seminarians and enabled them to give glory to God.

All the seminarians, dressed in their well-pressed, black house cassocks, were seated in the chapel for Holy Mass and the conclusion of their retreat. However, this Mass was special because His Eminence Cardinal Daniel Patrick Murphy, Archbishop of Baltimore, would be the celebrant.

As the procession of people started down the aisle, the seminarians stood and began singing:

Immaculate Mary, your praises we sing,
You reign now in splendor with Jesus our King.
Ave, Ave, Ave Maria, Ave, Ave Maria!

In heaven the blessed your glory proclaim.
On earth we your children invoke your
sweet name.
Ave, Ave, Ave Maria, Ave, Ave Maria!

We pray for the Church, our true Mother on earth,
And beg you to watch o'er the land of our birth.
Ave, Ave, Ave Maria, Ave, Ave Maria!

Luke, dressed in the robes of an altar server, processed down the aisle swinging the large incense thurible, which was casting a wide swath of smoke with the beautiful aroma of roses. It filled the grand chapel of Saint Peter's with the good and satisfying flavor of praising God.

Next came another seminarian, who was the acolyte. He was carrying a large golden crucifix that reflected the bright sunlight that was streaming through the elegant stained-glass windows. Six more seminarians, dressed in their cassock and surplice, followed. They were holding tall, white candles on golden stands.

A deacon, dressed in an alb and dalmatic, processed down the aisle holding high the Book of the Gospels, which was plated in a shining gold cover. He was followed by all the priests who taught at Saint Peter's. The last two priests were Father Kelly and Father Reynolds.

Finally, Cardinal Murphy, who was holding a golden shepherd's staff called a crozier and wearing a tall hat called a miter, processed down the aisle. He was followed by two more seminarians as the servers-- one for the crozier and one for the miter.

When Nicholas saw Cardinal Murphy dressed in his ceremonial attire and holding his crozier, he thought, *how beautiful the shepherd's golden staff is and what a powerful symbol it is of our bishop's authority. He has been sent by God to show us the way.*

Everyone took their proper places in the sanctuary of the chapel. The Cardinal, standing in front of the presider's chair, began, "In the name of the Father and of the Son and of the Holy Spirit! Peace be with you!"

All responded, "And with your spirit!"

The Mass continued with the entire assembly reciting the Confiteor:

"I confess to Almighty God and to you, my brothers and sisters, that I have greatly sinned in my thoughts and in my words, in what I have done and in what I have failed to do, through my fault, through my fault, through my most grievous fault; therefore, I ask blessed Mary ever-Virgin, all the Angels and Saints, and you, my brothers and sisters, to pray for me to the Lord, Our God."

All were seated to listen to the readings from the votive Mass for the Blessed Virgin Mary that the Cardinal was celebrating.

Once the readings were finished, Cardinal Murphy gave the deacon his blessing.

The deacon then proceeded to the ambo and in a clear, strong voice proclaimed, "A reading from the Holy Gospel according to Saint Luke: The angel Gabriel was sent from God to a town of Galilee called Nazareth, to a virgin betrothed to a man named Joseph, of the house of David, and the virgin's name was Mary. And coming to her, he said, '*Hail, full of grace! The Lord is with you.*'

"But she was greatly troubled at what was said and pondered what sort of greeting this might be. Then the angel said to her, '*Do not be afraid, Mary, for you have found favor with God. Behold, you will conceive in your womb and bear a son, and you shall name him Jesus. He will be great and will be called Son of the Most High, and the Lord God will give him the throne of David his father, and he will rule over the house of Jacob forever, and of his Kingdom there will be no end.*'

"But Mary said to the angel, '*How can this be, since I have no relations with a man?*' And the angel said to her in reply, '*The Holy Spirit will come upon you, and the power of the Most High will overshadow you. Therefore, the child to be born will be called holy, the Son of God. And behold, Elizabeth, your relative, has also conceived a son in her old age, and this is the sixth month for her who was called barren; for nothing will be impossible for God.*'

"Mary said, '*Behold, I am the handmaid of the Lord. May it be done to me according to your word.*' Then the angel departed from her.

"The Gospel of the Lord."

All were seated as Cardinal Daniel Patrick Murphy, who led the Archdiocese of Baltimore with joy and love for the Lord Jesus Christ, took his place at the ambo.

"A mother had to wake up her son for Sunday Mass. She knocks on the door of his room. *'Jimmy, it's time to get up. We have to go to Mass.'*

"On the other side of the door her son says, *'Oh, Mommy, I don't want to go to Mass.'*

"She bangs on the door harder. *'Jimmy, get up!'*

'Oh, Mommy, the kids, they don't like me, and their parents don't like me. It's boring and hot and takes forever. I don't want to go to Mass.'

'GET UP!'

'Mommy, you give me three good reasons why I should get up and go to Mass.'

'Okay, I will,' says his mother. *'First, it is Sunday, the Lord's day and we keep the commandments in this house and you are going to Mass. Second, you are forty-seven years old. And third, Jimmy, you're the priest.'*

The Cardinal smiled as the seminarians and faculty laughed. He then continued. "I wonder gentlemen if some priests are like Jimmy and approach holy Mass with the same attitude. Thank God, Our Blessed Mother did not take that attitude with the Archangel Gabriel. We all have days when we want to hide in bed and stay under the covers, but Jesus calls every one of us to action.

"Today in the Gospel, He calls Our Lady and she says, *'Yes.'* Mary is a role model for all of us. We must have faith to say, *'Yes'* to God, even when we don't understand every aspect of what He is asking. And as men of faith and one day as priests of faith, we will not avoid our responsibilities when confronted with them.

"Open your eyes, gentlemen. Take the time to notice what goes on around you. If there is a need, address it. If there is an injustice, challenge it. If there is pain, seek to comfort and help. What does Saint Francis teach us in his most famous prayer?

Lord, make me an instrument of your peace.
Where there is hatred, let me bring love.
Where there is offense, let me bring pardon.
Where there is discord, let me bring union.
Where there is error, let me bring truth.
Where there is doubt, let me bring faith.
Where there is despair, let me bring hope.
Where there is darkness, let me bring your light.
Where there is sadness, let me bring joy.

O Divine Master, let me not seek as much

To be consoled as to console,

To be understood as to understand,

To be loved as to love,

For it is giving that one receives,

It is in self-forgetting that one finds,

It is in pardoning that one is pardoned,

It is in dying that one is raised to eternal life.

"Gentlemen, Our Blessed Mother lived the principles of this prayer every day of her life on earth, and so should you and me. The Blessed Virgin is an instrument of God's peace. And so, you and I should follow her example as we begin this new school year. Make this your daily goal and prayer.

"We do not always know where God will send us or where he will place us, but always know that He is with you and will guide and help you even when things seem at their worst and the challenges seem overwhelming. God is there with us to guide and to help and to inspire us to be His most trusted and blessed servants.

"It is a gift and a privilege to be a priest, not a right. Work hard this year and strive to reach the high goals God is setting for each one of us. Keep His commandments with joy. Pray the Rosary every day. Our Lady will guide and help you. And always be merciful and generous. For remember, the measure with which you measure will be measured out to you. God Bless You."

Cardinal Murphy sat down while the deacon and the altar servers prepared the altar for the Liturgy of the Eucharist. When they were finished the Cardinal walked to the foot of the altar and received the gifts of bread and wine from two seminarians in the first row.

Now at the altar he said the Prayers of Thanksgiving to God for the gifts of bread and wine. Then taking the smoking thurible of incense from the deacon, he swung it over the gifts and the altar. Next came the ceremonial washing of the Cardinal's hands.

Everyone in the chapel stood when the Cardinal said, "Pray brethren that my sacrifice and yours may be acceptable to God, the almighty Father."

All responded, "May the Lord accept the sacrifice at your hands for the praise and glory of His name, for our good and the good of all His Holy Church."

All the priests joined Cardinal Murphy at the altar as he read the prayer over the offerings. It truly was a grand picture to see all the sacred ministers of the Church as they took part in the Holy Sacrifice of the Mass.

When he completed the prayer, the Cardinal said, "The Lord be with you."

"And with your Spirit," responded the seminarians.

"Lift up your hearts," said the Cardinal.

"We lift them up to the Lord!" responded the seminarians.

"Let us give thanks to the Lord our God," said the Cardinal.

"It is right and just," responded the seminarians.

Now everyone in the chapel sang: *Sanctus, Sanctus, Sanctus. Dominus Deus Sabaoth. Pleni sunt caeli et terra gloria tua. Hosana in excelsis. Benedictus qui venit in nominee Domini. Hosana in excelsis.*

Except for the priests and the Cardinal, all the seminarians knelt for the Eucharistic Prayer. This is the most powerful part of the Mass because at the hands of the Cardinal and the other priests, the bread and wine would become the Body and Blood of Our Lord, Jesus Christ.

Holding up the consecrated host, Cardinal Murphy said, *"Take this, all of you and eat of it, for this is my body, which will be given up for you."* All the concelebrating priests, with their right hands raised, quietly said the same words. The Cardinal then raised the consecrated host high. Placing the consecrated host on the paten that was on the altar, he genuflected, and all the priests bowed.

Taking the beautiful gold chalice in his hands, he said, *"Take this all of you and drink from it, for this is the chalice of my blood, the blood of the new and eternal covenant, which will be poured out for you and for many for the forgiveness of sins. Do this in memory of me."* All the concelebrating priests, with their right hands raised, said the words quietly. The Cardinal then raised the chalice high. Placing the chalice on the altar, he genuflected and all the priests bowed.

Cardinal Murphy continued with the Eucharistic Prayer. When it had ended, the deacon took the chalice and lifted it up at the same time that Cardinal Murphy lifted the consecrated host up. Now the Cardinal and all the priests chanted: *"Through him, with him and in him, O God, Almighty Father, in the unity of the Holy Spirit, all glory and honor is yours, now and forever!"*

"Amen," responded all the seminarians.

All the seminarians now stood and Cardinal Murphy led them in the *Lord's Prayer*, followed by the sign of peace.

Everyone then chanted:

Agnus Dei, quitollis peccata mundi: miserere nobis.

Agnus Dei, quitollis peccata mundi: miserere nobis.

Agnus Dei, quitollis peccata mundi: dona nobis pacem.

The seminarians knelt as the Cardinal said a silent prayer and then genuflected after raising the consecrated host over the chalice and pausing a few moments in silent adoration. Cardinal Murphy now exclaimed, *"Behold the Lamb of God, Behold Him who takes away the sins of the world, blessed are those called to the supper of the Lamb."*

Everyone responded, "Lord, I am not worthy that you should enter under my roof, but only say the word and my soul shall be healed."

Cardinal Murphy and the concelebrating priests received the Body of Our Lord in the Eucharist and the Blood of Our Lord from the chalice before the seminarians did.

When Nicholas returned to his pew he knelt and prayed in gratitude to God for all that he had been given. Instinctively, he then reached for the Miraculous Medal he wore and prayed to Our Lady. He asked her to guide and to help him and all the young men at Saint Peter's to become good and holy priests.

Mass ended when Cardinal Murphy recited the final prayers and gave the final blessing. As the Cardinal, priests, servers and deacon began to leave the altar, the seminarians stood up and everyone sang:

Hail Virgin of Virgins, thy praises we sing,
Thy throne is in heaven, thy Son is its King.
The saints and the angels thy glory proclaim,
All nations devoutly bow down at thy name.

Let all sing of Mary the Mystical Rod,
The Mirror of Justice, the Handmaid of God!
Let valley and mountain unite in her praise,
The sea with its waters the sun with its rays!

Let souls that are holy still holier be,
To sing with the angels Dear Mary of Thee!
Let all who are sinners to virtue return,
That hearts without number with thy love ever
Thy name is a power, thy love is a light,

We praise thee at morning, at noon and at night.
We thank thee, we bless thee, happy and free.
When tempted by Satan, we call upon thee!

Oh! Be thou Our Mother and pray to the Lord
That all may acknowledge and worship His word.
That good souls with courage may walk in His way
And sinners converted may join in His praise!

Chapter 7
The Banquet

It was the tradition at Saint Peter's High School Seminary that after the retreat in the beginning of the academic year the seminarians, along with the rector, vice rector and faculty, would share a special meal. This banquet took place in the grand Saint Peter's dining room. Unlike the cafeteria, this room was elegantly furnished with big, round oak tables and armchairs with upholstered seats and backs in a caramel color. Many beautiful religious pictures of the Blessed Virgin Mary, Saint Peter, Saint Paul and all the apostles hung on the walls. The big window that overlooked the manicured grounds of the seminary was framed by long, cranberry-colored crushed velvet drapes. A floor-to-ceiling red-brick fireplace with an ornate oak carved mantel and oak bookcases on both sides added to the elegance of the room.

The fact that His Eminence Cardinal Daniel P. Murphy, Archbishop of Baltimore, was the guest of honor at this dinner made it even more special for everyone present. There was much chatter and laughter as the boys filed in and took their places at the various tables. Nicholas and Jose spotted Luke and his roommate, Alan, and the four of them found a table where they all could sit together.

Silence enveloped the atmosphere as Cardinal Murphy, accompanied by Father Kelly and Father Reynolds, entered the dining room and made their way to the head table.

Every head bowed when Cardinal Murphy began, "In the name of the Father and of the Son and of the Holy Spirit. All powerful Father, we give you thanks for all we have, for everything, our lives and our hopes, come from you. We ask the powerful intercession of the Blessed Virgin Mary, the great Mother of God and Queen of Heaven, Saint Joseph and our patron, Saint Peter, and all the apostles whose images adorn this hall to intervene on our behalf and keep us safe from all attacks of the enemy.

"Bless us O Lord, and these your gifts, which we are about to receive from your bounty, through Christ Our Lord."

All responded, "Amen."

"May the King of everlasting glory make us partakers of the heavenly table."

All responded, "Amen."

"May the King of everlasting glory lead us to the banquet of life eternal."

All responded, "Amen."

"Saint Peter"

All responded, "Pray for us."

"In the name of the Father and of the Son and of the Holy Spirit."

All responded, "Amen."

The food for this meal was elegantly served on white porcelain plates. The first course consisted of a fresh garden salad with Italian dressing. A delicious aroma filled the dining room as the boys were served the main course—twice-baked potatoes, summer squash grown on the grounds of the seminary, parmesan crusted baked cod and Maryland's world-famous crab cakes. For dessert, Brother Antonio, their Franciscan cook, served his award-winning cheese cake topped with strawberry sauce and whipped cream.

What was very different about this banquet was the fact that the seniors were the waiters. They served Cardinal O'Malley and the priests sitting with him at the head table first, and then they served all their fellow seminarians. When everyone had been served, the seniors, carrying their own plates of food, proceeded to their assigned tables to enjoy the banquet, too.

This impressed Nicholas and he thought, *Yes, to serve rather than to be served. Like the prayer of Saint Francis in Cardinal Murphy's homily.*

The happy conversations of the boys filled the grand Saint Peter's dining room, along with the sound of the clinking of silverware and glasses. Father Reynolds told Brother Antonio that there must be some humility in this great feast. So instead of juice or milk, the boys drank water. A subtle but important point that Father Reynolds insisted upon.

Nicholas did not mind. He preferred the ice-cold water as it came from a spring on the seminary's grounds.

It was obvious by the smiles and laughter of Cardinal Murphy that he was truly enjoying himself at Saint Peter's. Finally, it came time for his departure. But before leaving, he made it a point to go from table to table with kind words of gratitude and encouragement to the seminarians on following the Will of God and discerning if they have been called to the beautiful vocation of the priesthood.

When the Cardinal approached the table that Nicholas was seated at Father Reynolds said, "Cardinal Murphy, I want you to meet Nicholas Gilroy and his roommate, Jose Romero."

Looking first at Jose, the Cardinal said, "Mr. Romero, I hear that you are bilingual and that Spanish is your second language. Your knowledge of Spanish may come in handy someday."

Turning to Nicholas, the Cardinal said, "Mr. Gilroy, I hear that you are a very good soccer player. Your knowledge of soccer may also come in handy someday."

Nicholas and Jose were so surprised with what the Cardinal had just said to them that they could not respond. And with looks of bewilderment on their faces, they stared at Cardinal Murphy as he walked away.

Before he left to follow the Cardinal, Father Reynolds said, "Gentlemen, I want both of you in my office in fifteen minutes."

Nicholas and Jose, confused and filled with anxiety, were unable to respond. As soon as Father Reynolds was no longer in the room, Luke — with a worried look on his face — said, "Boy, I hope you guys aren't in any trouble."

It was Jose in a serious tone who responded. "Well, if we are, we certainly could use some prayers."

✠

In some ways, the office of Father Stephen Reynolds was as imposing as the vice rector himself. The room had a massive oak bookcase and a large window that overlooked the inner courtyard with the beautiful statue of Our Lady of Mount Carmel. It also had a desk that was large enough to accommodate the file folders that were neatly stacked on one side and the laptop computer and telephone that was on the other side.

Impressive pictures of the Sacred Heart of Jesus and the Immaculate Heart of Mary hung on one wall, along with a large wooden hand-carved crucifix. On the other wall were two other pictures, one of the current Pope and one of Cardinal Daniel P. Murphy, Archbishop of Baltimore. A large statue of Our Lady of Guadalupe was on a small table in the corner. All this was a reminder to visitors that this, indeed, was the office of a Catholic priest.

Nicholas and Jose stood at the entrance waiting to be asked in. Because the door to the office was open, they could see Father Reynolds seated behind his desk reading what appeared to be a letter.

Noticing the boys, Father Reynolds said in an inviting tone, "Gentlemen, please come in and sit down."

Two wooden chairs had been positioned in front of the desk. Over the years, many seminarians had found themselves seated in those chairs. Usually it was because they had to be disciplined. So, it was natural for Nicholas and Jose to be a little nervous when they were summoned by Father Reynolds to his office.

"Gentlemen are you familiar with a program called student exchange?"

"Yes, I am," Jose answered. "Many students in Puerto Rico become exchange students. It allows them to travel to different countries of the world, to learn different cultures and sometimes to learn a new language. We also welcome many exchange students from other countries to our hospitals and universities in Puerto Rico who want to study Spanish."

"Very good, Mr. Romero," Father Reynolds cheerfully replied.

"We also have a relationship here at Saint Peter's with various high school seminaries around the world. We have received a request from a school in Mexico that they would like to have two of our students from Saint Peter's take part in their student exchange program. The name of the school is Saint Juan Diego High School Seminary and it is in the city of San Miguel de Allende. I will also be going, as I have been asked to join the faculty and teach English and Introduction to the Catechism for this academic year.

"We have discussed what students would be going among ourselves as faculty and with Cardinal Murphy, since he is the one who has to approve this exchange. It has been decided that the two of you will accompany me to Mexico."

Nicholas, who had never traveled much, even in the United States, was taken by surprise. A little worried about spending his sophomore year in Mexico, he blurted out, "Father, will it be safe for us in Mexico. I have read and seen images on the internet that are a little scary."

"Have no fear," Father Reynolds assured him. "We will be taking part in a program of educational and cultural learning. However, the two of you do have a record of going off on your own from time to time. Remember your freshman year when you filled Saint Peter's with men that were homeless. Going off on your own will not be permitted on this trip."

"I am happy we were able to help those men," Nicholas said honestly. "I think it was what Jesus would want us to do."

"Yes, I agree," Jose added.

"Well, gentlemen, the faculty also agrees with you. Your imaginative approach in helping those men who were homeless put you on the top of the list for this program. You have good hearts and there will be ample opportunity in Mexico to be of service to those in need."

"We will have to tell our families," Nicholas responded.

"Already done. All we need is your approval, gentlemen. This program is voluntary. If you wish to stay here at Saint Peter's you are welcome to do so, but I would urge both of you to take part in this program. It will be a wonderful opportunity for you."

Smiling, Nicholas and Jose looked at each other. Then they both turned to Father Reynolds and Jose said without hesitation, "When do we leave?"

"Yes!" exclaimed Nicholas. "When do we leave?"

Chapter 8
Welcome to Mexico

Padre Enrique Ramirez, standing in the welcoming area of the airport, intensely observed every passenger getting off the airplane.

Waving his hands, he shouted, "Padre, over here," when he saw Father Reynolds, Nicholas and Jose.

The trio quickly headed toward Padre Ramirez, who, with a wide smile on his face, said, "Welcome to Mexico!"

Father Reynolds responded, "Boys, I want you to meet Father or as they say here in Mexico, Padre Enrique Ramirez, rector of Saint Juan Diego High School Seminary." He then introduced Nicholas and Jose to Padre Rivera.

"I speak for all the staff and seminarians. We are so happy that you have decided to spend your sophomore year with us. Over the years, we have had many exchange students from Saint Peter's and many students from Saint Juan Diego have gone to your seminary. And, of course, it is an honor to have Padre Reynolds on our teaching staff this academic year. Now let's get you settled in as soon as possible."

As Padre Enrique Ramirez led the way to the baggage claim area, Nicholas's mind was swirling, trying to comprehend what the many voices around him were saying in Spanish.

Jose must have sensed his friend's confusion because he said, "Don't worry, amigo. I know what they are saying, and I'll make sure you don't get into any trouble."

All the other times that Jose said something about making sure that Nicholas didn't get into any trouble, he was joking. But this time Jose was serious, and Nicholas felt a sense of relief and some comfort.

As they walked to where Padre Ramirez had parked his car, they were almost blinded by the sun, which was very bright and very hot. Seated in the air-conditioned vehicle, Father Reynolds, Nicholas and Jose began to relax. With a sense of adventure, they now looked forward to the two-hour drive to the city of San Miguel de Allende, where the high school seminary was located.

Getting up at five in the morning to make sure they had plenty of time to board the plane in Baltimore, and then the two-hour stopover in Texas made for a long trip. All three were exhausted and wanted to just relax and look out the windows of the car at their new surroundings.

It didn't take long before the airport and the city were left far behind. For miles all they saw was a flat sandy terrain with an occasional patch of grassy land. Cactuses were sprouting like mushrooms all over the place. Some were low to the ground and some were as tall as trees. Some of the tall cactuses had tops that looked like pincushions, and many of the cactuses close to the ground had beautiful white, yellow, red, purple or orange flowers. As they continued on the highway, the flat land began to change into hillsides and then into rugged mountains.

Nicholas, who had not traveled much in the United States and had never been in another country, was delighted and in awe at what he was seeing. He thought, *Thank you, God, for this beautiful land, for You are the Creator of all things.*

When the car began its descent down into the valley, Padre Ramirez exclaimed, "Only about thirty minutes more and we will be at San Miguel de Allende."

Father Reynolds said, "When I knew we were coming here, I had Nicholas and Jose look up information on the internet about your city."

Nicholas chimed in, "Yes, and I can't wait to see it because I read that it won an award for being one of the best cities in the world."

"Yes, that was a great honor for my city and it made us very proud. You will see for yourselves how unique and beautiful it is. But first I want to tell you how my city got its name.

"In the year 1542, a Franciscan friar from Spain by the name of Juan de San Miguel came to Mexico to start a mission so that he could help the native people who lived in this valley. The legend of the founding of our city is that the first place he settled was near a river. Unfortunately, the river often went dry. Now Friar Juan owned two big dogs. One day when the river went dry the two hot and thirsty dogs wandered away from the mission. Friar Juan went out into the wilderness to search for them. When he found his two dogs, they were reclining next to a spring of water. So, Friar Juan moved his mission to that spring of water, and he named the town San Miguel.

"Then in the year 1826 the name of the town was changed to San Miguel de Allende to honor a hero who was born here, Ignacio Allende. He was one of the leaders in the uprising to free Mexico from Spanish rule. He was captured and then executed because of his role in this movement."

Making their way down the main street of the historic center of town, they passed four giant statues of prominent men of San Miguel de Allende, one of them of Ignacio Allende. In the middle of these statues of important men was the statue of Saint Michael the Archangel. Padre Ramirez found a place to park and everyone got out of the car.

Padre Ramirez, acting as their guide, said, "In the eighteenth century our town became very rich by providing supplies to the men who lived and worked in the silver mining camps. All the large mansions, palaces and churches that you see were built during that time. The town also was the home of many wealthy hacienda owners and was one of the most important and prosperous settlements in New Spain with a population of 30,000 people."

The historic area was a mix of residential and commercial establishments. About half of the colonial buildings had been converted into stores, restaurants, art galleries and hotels. There were no parking meters, no traffic signals and no fast-food restaurants.

The narrow cobblestone lanes were lined with houses built of stone and sunbaked bricks. Painted in various colors, the houses had bougainvillea vines with pink, purple, orange, yellow and white flowers falling down on the outside.

Padre Ramirez said, "There are about two thousand of these colorful houses and behind each one of them are courtyards with beautiful gardens of various sizes."

Entering a lovely park in the center of town, looming before them was a spectacular site — the castle-like structure, La Parroquia de San Miguel Arcangel or in English, the Church of Saint Michael the Archangel. It was a magnificent church, pink in color with neo-Gothic towers soaring silently and powerfully into the sky. There was something magical as the movement of the sun illuminated the church and it began to change into different colors.

As Father Reynolds, Nicholas and Jose gazed in awe at the massive church, Padre Ramirez said, "Yes, San Miguel Arcangel is very impressive and it does draw us closer to God and all of His glory. But what is even more impressive and is a testimony of the power of God is the fact that the person who designed and built this magnificent church was a local bricklayer who had no formal architectural skills or technical training."

Nicholas was so happy with the many new sights and sounds he had seen his first day in Mexico. Looking up at the magnificent fairy-tale structure he silently prayed: *Our Lady of Guadalupe, please help me bring glory to your Son while I am here in Mexico and Saint Michael the Archangel please protect me, Father Reynolds, Jose, and all the people of San Miguel de Allende.*

Chapter 9
Saint Juan Diego High School Seminary

Saint Juan Diego High School Seminary rose before them like a towering mountain of brick and adobe. The solid columns of red brick framing the doors of the main entrance were a dramatic contrast to the white brick adobe-style building. Situated on twenty acres, it was strategically located about a mile from the historic center of the city. It was four stories high and designed for many hundreds of seminarians. Nicholas thought, *Wow, it's even bigger than Saint Peter's.*

Upon entering the building, Father Reynolds, Nicholas and Jose were pleasantly surprised to see that it had a beautiful inner courtyard with terracotta tile walkways surrounded by a grass-covered yard with many bushes and flowering plants that were perfectly manicured. This place of quiet retreat had numerous lime trees that filled the air with a sweet-smelling citrus aroma. Some of these trees were over ten feet tall and provided much-needed shade from the bright Mexican sun.

As they made their way to the chapel at the end of the courtyard, they all stopped. In the center of the courtyard were bigger-than-life marble statues of Mary, John and Mary Magdalene looking up at the statue of Jesus on the cross. It was a powerful moment for the three of them as they pondered Our Lord's sacrifice to redeem us from sin and the terrible pain that Our Lady had to endure.

The white brick adobe chapel was very simple on the outside. However, everyone who entered for the first time was astonished. This sacred space was large enough to hold one thousand worshippers and had many rows of polished wooden pews. Shiny green and gray marble tiles covered the floor.

The sanctuary was large with a row of pews on both sides that faced each other so that the seminarians at certain times during the day could pray the Divine Office. A Baroque, twenty-four-karat, gold-plated tabernacle was in the center of the sanctuary. Six scenes from the life of Christ graced the front of the tabernacle, and on each corner at the top were statuettes of the four Evangelists.

Situated above the tabernacle was a huge mosaic that ran the length of the sanctuary and went up to the ceiling. This breath-taking mosaic was handcrafted of many colorful marble mosaic tiles and was a picture of Our Lady of Guadalupe and Saint Juan Diego.

As Nicholas and Jose gazed in awe at the beautiful picture, Father Reynolds exclaimed, "Juan Diego was a peasant living in Mexico. In December of 1531 he was on his way to Holy Mass when a radiant woman appeared to him. In his native tongue she introduced herself as the Mother of God.

"Mary then told Juan to go to his bishop and tell him that the Mother of God wanted him to build a chapel in her honor on Tepeyac Hill, which had been the site of a pagan temple. So, Juan went to his bishop and told him what Mary had said, but he didn't believe him. On his way back home, Mary appeared to him again. After telling her what had happened, Juan then told Mary that he was just a poor man and that perhaps she should send someone more important who would be a better messenger. But Mary insisted that it had to be him.

"Juan went back to his bishop, who demanded that some proof be given that he was telling the truth. Juan again went back to Tepeyac Hill, where Mary was waiting for him. After telling her that his bishop wanted proof that he was telling the truth, she agreed and told Juan to tell his bishop that he would get his proof the next day.

"But the next day, Juan's uncle became very sick and he went instead to find a priest. On the way, Mary appeared to him and he told her what had happened. Mary promised Juan that his uncle would be healed. She then told him to climb up the hill and gather the roses that were blooming there. But it was December and roses do not bloom in December. The Blessed Virgin Mary arranged the roses herself in Juan Diego's cloak, called a tilma. She then told him to take them to his bishop.

"Juan thought that the miracle would be the roses in December, but when he opened his tilma the roses fell on the floor and imprinted on his tilma was the miraculous image of Our Lady of Guadalupe. News of Our Lady's apparitions caused a wave of nearly 3,000 Indians a day to convert to the Christian faith.

"That chapel was then built, and it is the great Cathedral in Mexico City. When Catholics were being persecuted in the Mexican Revolution in the beginning of the twentieth century, non-believers attempted to destroy the tilma with an explosive. The altar, the marble steps and the Cathedral's windows were all heavily damaged, but the pane of glass that protected Juan Diego's tilma with the image of Our Lady was not even cracked. To this day the tilma is perfectly preserved; and to this day, there have been countless numbers of miracles attributed to the intercession of Our Lady of Guadalupe.

Turning to Nicholas and Jose, Father Reynolds ended by saying, "If we are humble and obedient to Our Lady like Saint Juan Diego, we will have nothing to fear because Our Lady will always be with us to guide and to protect us."

Chapter 10
Called to Serve

Even though Saint Juan Diego High School Seminary was bigger and had more students than Saint Peter's, the friendly outreach of the seminarians and faculty made Nicholas and Jose feel right at home. Nicholas, although homeschooled until a little over a year ago, felt humbled and grateful that he had been chosen from all the other boys at Saint Peter's to spend his sophomore year in Mexico getting to know the people and their customs. He knew that this experience would help him minister to all people when he became a Catholic priest.

The first couple of weeks were like a whirlwind of excitement and curiosity for Nicholas. Since all the boys at Saint Juan Diego were taught the English language, they were eager to engage in conversations with the two seminarians from America to improve their English. In fact, Nicholas and Jose soon became very popular. Many of the seminarians went out of their way to help them, and many spent their leisure time with them so that they could learn what it was like to live in the United States. They would ask many questions about seminary life in Baltimore.

On the other hand, Nicholas was also becoming more adept at speaking Spanish because he was being tutored twice a week by Pedro, who was a senior at Saint Juan Diego. Nicholas even gave Pedro the nickname, Guardian Angel, and told him about Gabe Anderson, who also was a senior and had helped him his first year at Saint Peter's. Then, of course, he had Jose, his personal translator, if he got confused about what someone was saying in Spanish. Jose joked that Nicholas was really getting ready for ever-lasting life, as everyone in Heaven spoke Spanish.

Nicholas also was pleasantly surprised how much he enjoyed Mexican food. In fact, so far there was nothing that he had eaten that he disliked. His favorite dishes were chicken quesadillas, chicken tortilla soup, shredded pork tacos and savory fried beef empanadas. He loved the homemade cinnamon-sugared churros that were dipped in a chocolate sauce and were similar to American doughnuts, but tasted even better. His favorite dessert was a delicate baked custard called flan. It came in different flavors such as orange or chocolate and was topped with a sweet caramel sauce.

Pedro told him that flan was a popular dessert in Spain and was brought to Mexico by the conquistador Hernando Cortes in 1518.

For Father Reynolds, his time in Mexico was like being on a sabbatical, a time away from all the responsibilities he had at Saint Peter's. Teaching only two courses, one on the Introduction of the Catechism and another on speaking and writing in English, was a marked change from his duties as vice rector. He now had more free time for prayer and spiritual reading. It also gave him the opportunity to minister as a priest to the community of people who lived near Saint Juan Diego. This allowed him to grow closer to Christ as he met his Lord and Savior in the good people of San Miguel de Allende.

Father Reynolds began to remember his own days in the seminary as he watched Nicholas and Jose, and the Mexican seminarians interacting and learning new things about each other's cultures, and also about the universality of the Catholic Church. How he had enjoyed his days as a seminarian. But now being a priest was even better. He thought, *The Church can be found on every continent. God is at work to bring all His children home to the Catholic Church.*

Since Father Reynolds was responsible for Nicholas and Jose while in Mexico, he made sure they knew he was always available if they needed him for any reason. He met with them twice a week to mentor them spiritually and to help them adjust to their new environment. He would meet with both Nicholas and Jose in one of these mentoring sessions. The other mentoring session, he would meet with each boy separately.

The weekly meetings with both Nicholas and Jose always took place when they had finished breakfast after attending Sunday morning Mass. Even though it was the middle of October, today felt like a summer day back home as Nicholas and Jose jogged through the courtyard to the place where Father Reynolds was waiting.

The time together in Mexico had made the boys grow even closer together. In fact, for Nicholas, Jose was like the brother he never had. Many times, he would say, "Sorry Jose, now you have another brother. Me!"

Because they shared the call by Christ to be priests, Jose felt the same way — closer to Nicholas than to his own biological brothers.

And Jose would always respond, "And you are becoming my favorite brother, as long as you do as I say! Just remember who is the boss around here!"

As Nicholas and Jose approached him, Father Reynolds thought, *what fine young men of God they are becoming.*

In unison, Nicholas and Jose cried out with enthusiasm, "Good morning Father."

"Good morning gentlemen." Father Reynolds then led them to a patio table with chairs under one of the tall lime trees.

"Boys," he began, "the other day Padre Ramirez brought me to the Home of the Holy Family. It is an orphanage that has about one hundred boys, ages one to seventeen. It is run by Mother Teresa's religious order, the Missionaries of Charity.

"As you know, Mother Teresa's Sisters are known all over the world for the wonderful work that they do for the poor and the abandoned. They also have a strong spirituality and have a great love and devotion to Our Lord, Jesus Christ. Because of this love, it is important for them to start every day with the Holy Sacrifice of the Mass. While I am here, I have offered to help their parish priests in celebrating Mass for them at their chapel three times a week.

"There are seven Sisters, including the Mother Superior, and they do a tremendous job in taking care of these boys. The only other help they receive are from the three women from town who are paid to cook, clean and do the boys' laundry, a few Franciscan brothers who freely help them with the education of the boys, and a handyman who is paid very little in exchange for his living there. But they still can use a little help. As future priests, this would be a wonderful opportunity for you to use the talents that God has given you and help these boys. And as young men of prayer, it would leave a lasting impression on them. And who knows, maybe you will even inspire vocations."

"Father," Nicholas quietly asked, "Why would so many boys be orphaned? Did all their parents die?"

"There are many reasons why one might become an orphan. Some of the boys were abandoned, others were given up because their parents could not afford to care for them. And, yes, others became orphans due to the death of their parents. At least for those who gave them up, they gave them a chance at life.

"In our country, and even in this one, many take a more drastic and evil approach by killing their child through abortion. We must thank God for the grace He gave those parents to choose life. Always remember, the belief in the dignity of the human person is at the heart of our theology. Every person is made in the image and likeness of God and thus deserves both life and freedom and justice to thrive and follow God's plan for them."

"Thinking of the orphaned boys makes me appreciate my mother and father even more," Jose mused. "I am so happy my parents always gave me and my siblings support and love."

"And many prayers," Nicholas added.

Father Reynolds continued, "Jose, because you are bilingual, I thought that you could help teach English. Many of the Sisters come from English-speaking countries and they are already teaching the boys English. But having someone their age to interact with them and speak English would be of tremendous value to them. Nicholas, you can also help by teaching the boys how to speak and write the English words that you have been learning in Spanish.

"The Sisters do try to give the boys some physical education. Nicholas, I thought that maybe you could coach them in soccer. Maybe even having them form teams so that they could play games against each other. Jose, you will also help the boys since I know that you are well-versed in soccer, or should I say football.

"Now, of course, you don't have to do this if you feel you are not able to handle this assignment, for it will take up a lot of your time and energy."

Smiling, both Nicholas and Jose exclaimed in unison, "When do we start?"

Chapter 11
Home of the Holy Family

Nicholas was overcome with joy when Father Reynolds announced that after lunch, he was going to drive him and Jose to meet Sister Monica, Mother Superior, at the Home of the Holy Family. It took only about fifteen minutes to reach the orphanage, which was on the outskirts of the city. The compound consisted of six long ranch-style adobe buildings, which were in a semicircle with a white adobe mission-style chapel in the center.

As Father Reynolds and the boys were getting out of the parked car, a man wearing loose fitting cotton pants, a cotton shirt of many colors, and a vest and boots made of leather walked up to them. His dark brown eyes, long brown hair, and olive face with long side-burns and a neatly trimmed mustache were shielded from the sun by the wide-brimmed sombrero that he was wearing.

"Boys," said Father Reynolds, "I want you to meet Pablo. He is the caretaker of Holy Family. He helps and takes care of the Sisters and the boys, and he can fix anything."

Pablo said, "Padre Reynolds, good to see you again. Have you brought more boys for Mother Monica to care for?"

Laughing, Father Reynolds replied, "Oh no, Pablo. This is Nicholas Gilroy and Jose Romero. They came with me from the United States and they are staying at Saint Juan Diego High School Seminary as exchange students this school year. They are studying to become Catholic priests. Sister Monica told me that she could use some help and these boys are eager to help her.

"Oh, yes, Padre. With so many boys we could use all the help we can get."

Now looking intently at Nicholas and Jose, he continued, "You have chosen well, I think. Even if I don't understand and follow your religion. Amigos, now follow me. Mother Monica is waiting for you."

As he followed this stranger, Nicholas thought, *Wow, he looks like a real Mexican Cowboy. And it certainly is clear that he isn't Catholic. I wonder why he is working here?*

Pablo brought them to a ranch house that was next to the chapel and knocked. A petite, middle-age woman opened the door. On her feet were sandals and she was dressed in the habit of the Missionaries of

Charity — a white cotton sari with three blue stripes over a long, loose white garment. Her face was framed with a blue and white cotton head scarf. Mother Teresa, who was the founder of this religious order, picked the color, blue, because it represents the Virgin Mary.

In a crisp English accent that is typical of educated people born in India, she said with a smile, "Father Reynolds, it is good to see you again. The Sisters and I are looking forward to your Masses in our chapel. And I see that you have brought with you the two young men who will be helping us."

"Yes, Sister Monica, this is Nicholas Gilroy and Jose Romero."

"Please, you can address me as Mother Monica."

Nicholas was full of gratitude and hope that he was going to help these Sisters. He knew that Mother Teresa's Sisters are known all over the world for their work in helping the poor, the sick and the dying, the abandoned and the orphans, and the addicted and the abused. *This is really the work that Jesus speaks about in Matthew 23,* thought Nicholas.

Nicholas spoke first, "Mother Monica, it is a privilege to be able to help you with the boys who live here."

In his eagerness to help, Jose asked, "When do we start?"

Laughing, Mother Monica said, "Please come inside. Before I put you to work, there is someone I want all of you to meet."

She led them down a small hallway and opened a door on the left-hand side. On the wall there was a crucifix and a framed picture of Mother Teresa. A large, pine table with six simple chairs were the only furniture in the room. And in one of the chairs was a young man who seemed to be about the same age as Nicholas and Jose.

The young man immediately got out of the chair as Mother Monica said, "I want you to meet Javier Santiago. Javier is a senior at Saint Thomas Aquinas Academy, a private Catholic high school in San Miguel de Allende. This is the second year that he has been coming to Holy Family. He comes twice a week to help us with our boys. Javier also has been very successful in raising money for us through various fund raisers at his high school. Javier, this is Father Reynolds. And these are the two seminarians that I told you about, Nicholas Gilroy and Jose Romero."

With a nod of his head, he first addressed Father Reynolds. "It is a pleasure to meet you, Father." Then, looking intensely at the boys, he said, "Mother Monica has told me that you are studying to be Catholic priests. It is an honor to be able to help you here at Holy Family Home."

Both Nicholas and Jose were surprised by Javier's words.

Smiling and full of gratitude for these three young men that God had sent to help her with the boys in the orphanage, Mother Monica said, "Before Javier takes you around the compound and Father Reynolds and I discuss the schedule and details of how the three of you will be working together, let us spend some time with Our Lord and ask Him to give us the strength and guidance so that everything we do will bring glory to Him."

All of them followed Mother Monica back into the hallway where she opened the door on the right-hand side. Scattered on the floor were square mats that were used as kneelers. On a small table in the center of one of the walls was a plain, wooden tabernacle with a golden door.

Taking a key from her pocket, Mother Monica unlocked the tabernacle door. Genuflecting, she then took out a monstrance containing the Holy Eucharist and placed it on the table in front of the tabernacle. Everyone then knelt on a mat in silent prayer, praising and adorating Our Lord.

Nicholas immediately sensed the strong and True Presence of Jesus in the Holy Eucharist. It felt like a warm loving light was shining on him and then a deep peace came over him as he silently prayed, *Loving Father, thank you for bringing me here. Help me to do your work without fear or distraction. Thank you and praise you. Everything I have are gifts from You. Help me to use my gifts well in helping these Missionaries of Charity.*

Chapter 12
The Three Amigos

Father Reynolds and Mother Monica had arranged that every Tuesday and Thursday after their classes, Nicholas and Jose would go to the Holy Family Home. They would spend two hours teaching English and sports to the boys who lived there. They were eager and very excited to begin their mission, especially since Javier Santiago was picking them up after he finished his classes at Saint Thomas Aquinas Academy.

The academy, which was affiliated with and taught by Dominican Friars, was a private boy's Catholic high school in San Miguel de Allende with an enrollment of about one thousand students. Many wealthy families from all over the area sent their sons there. The college-preparatory academy excelled in academics and in sports, particularly soccer.

As the new silver metallic four-wheel-drive vehicle pulled up to the waiting boys, Jose poked Nicholas and said, "This sure beats peddling our bikes all over the place."

"Yes, but it did keep us humble," responded Nicholas, although he, too, was happy to see Javier and the car in which they would be riding.

"I know, but humility does not keep you dry when it is raining," Jose said, grinning.

"Maybe a little rain on you wouldn't be such a bad idea," Nicholas retorted.

Through the open window Javier shouted, "Hey guys, let's get going!"

Jose, always ready to take charge, bowed and said, "After you."

As soon as Nicholas was seated in the passenger side and Jose was seated in the back, Javier took off.

Jose spoke first. "Wow, this is some car! With powerful wheels like this you can handle any difficult terrain with ease."

"Yes, you are right, but I didn't want or need so expensive a car. This was a surprise from my father, who always wants me to have the best. He means well, but things don't bring you happiness and sometimes they take you away from what Our Lord wants you to do," responded Javier.

"That is so true," Nicholas agreed. "Back in the United States we are blessed with many material things: food, clothes, smartphones, tablets, computers, you name it. And none of those things matter if they do not, in some way, give glory to God."

"And you see it on television," Jose chimed in. "The TV ads all make you believe that you have to have new things, the best things, the most expensive things. Yet none of that is important. My mom would take us to the goodwill store; and you know what, I found many good clothes for only a few dollars. Now if I went to a store in the mall or bought them from the internet it would have cost ten times the amount or more!"

Javier, responding to both Nicholas and Jose, said, "Yes, I agree with you. There is great value in a simple life."

Nicholas out of curiosity asked Javier, "What is your father like?"

Javier frowned and said, "He can be a difficult man. I know he loves me, but he is always worrying about money and trying to make more money. Money does not make you happy in the long run. Trust me on that."

"What is your school like?" Jose then asked.

"The academy is one of the best schools in Mexico. It has good teachers and is very expensive. I know I am getting a good education and I am grateful. But many days I wonder what it would be like to be in a school with regular kids rather than the kids from wealthy families. Money breeds a different culture, one of entitlement."

"You don't seem to suffer from that, my friend!" Jose responded. "In fact, you seem rather humble for the son of a wealthy man."

"You are most kind, Jose. But I need to learn more humility if I am to serve God the way I should. That is why I help the boys at Holy Family Home."

Nicholas was surprised to hear Javier speak of the importance of humility and serving God so he had the courage to ask, "Javier, have you ever considered becoming a priest?"

Javier responded, "Can you both keep a secret?"

"Yes," Nicholas and Jose quickly responded.

Pausing and mustering the courage to continue, Javier's voice began to quiver as he said, "I have felt called to be a Catholic priest since I was a small boy. I love the Mass, I love to pray, and I love to serve God by serving others. But my father would never allow me to become a priest. He would say that being a priest is a poor career choice and a waste of time, and that the world needs more successful men of business and not more poverty-stricken priests looking for handouts. If you want money, go and work for it, he would say."

Javier's voice filled with emotion and with tears in his eyes said, as if he was praying, "I so want to be a Catholic priest!"

Nicholas was moved with such compassion that he placed his hand on Javier's shoulder. "All things are possible, Javier, through God. Keep praying and keep asking Our Lord to guide you and for Our Blessed Mother to pray for you; and if it is the Will of God, you will become a Catholic priest."

So much had been said and there was so much to ponder that the three companions were silent for the rest of the drive to the orphanage.

It was only after parking his car that Javier broke the silence, "Okay guys, follow me. We always check in first with Pablo, and I know where to find him."

In the back of one of the ranch houses that served as a dormitory for the boys there was a barn. The barn was where the Sisters kept their only car and where an enclosed area served as Pablo's living and sleeping quarters.

As the three boys approached, a short-haired, brown and white medium-size dog came running toward them with its tail wagging. And right behind the dog was Pablo.

Javier petted the friendly dog and said, "Nicholas and Jose, this is Perrito and he is a very special dog. For he is loved by all the boys who live here."

"Yes, Perrito is a very special dog," exclaimed Pablo. "I found him hiding behind a big rock and he was so little. So, I named him Perrito, which means little dog. He loves all the boys here because he is one of them, an orphan. Coyotes killed his mama. When I take my walk at night to make sure everyone is safe, Perrito is with me and guards us all."

His voice full of enthusiasm, Nicholas said, "Oh, Pablo, Father Reynolds does the same thing every night back home that you do. He walks the halls of Saint Peter's Seminary. But instead of a dog for protection, Father prays his Rosary to Our Lady for our protection."

"Yes, Our Lady of Guadalupe, she is most holy," Pablo agreed.

"I can give you some rosary beads if you don't have any, and then you, too, can pray to Our Lady for protection as you take your nightly walks with Perrito," responded Nicholas.

With a tone of sadness in his voice, Pablo said, "No, Amigo, Our Lady of Guadalupe listens to your Padre Reynolds, but she would never listen to me."

"You're wrong Pablo," Nicholas quickly responded. "Why would you think that? Our Lady loves all of us."

With a forlorn look in his eyes, Pablo just shook his head and Nicholas said no more.

As they approached the building that was used as the school, a boy about eleven years old came running out. "Javier, Javier, are these the two Americans that Mother Monica told us about?"

It was clear that this boy with dark wavy hair, big brown eyes flashing with anticipation and a smile so wide that his teeth were showing, was extremely happy to see Javier, and he gave him a big hug.

"Yes, Miguel. This is Nicholas Gilroy and Jose Romero and they will be helping the boys here with their English. But maybe even more important than this, they will be helping me with teaching you and the boys how to play sports, especially your favorite."

"You mean soccer?" Miguel was so excited that he began jumping up and down.

Pablo immediately took over. "Now Miguel, let's calm down. You know the rules. You should not be here but inside with all the other boys." Turning to Nicholas and Jose, Pablo continued, "Oh, this is Miguel and as you can see, he is very happy to meet you."

"We are also happy to meet you," exclaimed Jose with a big smile and then he gave Miguel a hug.

"Yes, Miguel, I, too, am very happy to meet you," Nicholas added.

Meeting Miguel made Nicholas want to help all the boys who lived at Holy Family more than ever. However, he couldn't get out of his mind that Pablo felt Our Blessed Mother didn't love him and he didn't know how to help him.

Chapter 13
The Soccer Saints

Not only did Nicholas, Jose and Javier all feel that God was calling them to the priesthood, they also had another thing in common. They all loved the sport of soccer. Nicholas began playing soccer when he was seven years old. Jose began playing as a young boy in Puerto Rico before he moved to the United States, and Javier began playing when he was in the first grade. All three were pretty good, especially Javier, who was instrumental in helping his high school win many championship games against rival schools.

Loving the game of soccer and being a good player is one thing, but to be in charge with the responsibility of organizing the boys at the orphanage into competing teams was an extremely daunting task. The three boys were determined to come up with the best possible strategy to accomplish this.

The age of the boys at Holy Family ranged from as young as one to as old as seventeen. It was decided that any boy four years old or younger could not be on a team. Next it was decided that Holy Family would have three levels of soccer in which the boys would be placed according to their age.

Jose volunteered to work with the younger boys, ages five to nine. The next level would be middle school boys, ages ten to thirteen, and Nicholas felt that he would like to work with them. Since Javier was a senior and captain of his soccer team at Saint Thomas Aquinas Academy, he was the best choice to work with the boys in high school.

A soccer game is played with two teams, and each team is allowed a minimum of seven and up to eleven players on the field at one time, one of whom is a goal keeper. There were enough boys at Holy Family to have two teams for each of the three levels. This way they would be able to play matches against each other.

Nicholas came up with the idea of having each of the three levels of players be called by a saint's name. Nicholas felt that this would be a wonderful way for the boys to pray before each match to that saint for protection on the field, and in every aspect of their lives. With a little research he came up with three saints to whom soccer players have been known to pray to.

Jose wanted his boys to be called the Saint Luigi Soccer Players after Luigi Scrosoppi, an Italian priest who was known for his dedication to the youth. He encouraged them to take part in sports, especially soccer, and in pictures he is depicted holding a soccer ball.

Nicholas wanted his boys to be called the Saint John Paul II Soccer Players after Pope John Paul II. When he was a young boy growing up in Poland the future pope, Karol Wojtyla, played soccer. He had the position of goal keeper in the games.

Javier wanted his boys to be called the Saint Pier Giorgio Soccer Players after Pier Giorgio Frassati who was born in Italy. Even as a young boy, he had a love for the poor. Many times, he would give them money, bring them food or supply them with medicine. He arranged hiking trips with his friends in the mountains where it served as an opportunity to lead them to Mass, reading the Bible and praying Our Lady's Rosary. And playing a soccer game was always a part of his plan.

Nicholas knew that this was the perfect saint for Javier's team. Like Javier, Pier Giorgio came from a wealthy family and his father also did not want him to be a Catholic priest. Nicholas told Javier to pray to this saint for his help so that the heart of his father would be changed. Nicholas said that he, too, would also pray to Pier Giorgio for this.

The boys at the orphanage were eager and happy to play; therefore, organizing them into the different teams was not difficult. Besides, many of the boys had been playing soccer among themselves, but not in an organized way. The biggest obstacle was the lack of equipment. None of the boys had soccer cleats, soccer socks, shin guards, soccer balls or goal frames.

Javier came to the rescue with the basics. He bought each team a new soccer ball, and was able to get two older goal frames that were rusted and had holes in the netting that his school was planning to throw out. Nicholas couldn't help notice that Javier was becoming more and more like Saint Pier Giorgio.

Nicholas began with covering the basics. "Kicking the soccer ball, the right way is important," he instructed his team. "One mistake that we all make when we first start playing the game of soccer is kicking the ball with our toes rather than with the top part of our foot. Now this is how you kick the ball." Nicholas used the top of his foot to kick the soccer ball, sending it sailing with a good amount of power and drive. "See how you can send the ball forward easily."

He then lined the boys up and, one at a time, they practiced kicking the ball. Nicholas wanted to teach his boys sportsmanship, and at the same time make the game of soccer fun. He wanted to give all his boys a chance to play and felt that team building was more important right now. He encouraged their efforts by exclaiming, "Good job" or "That's better."

Nicholas looked forward to working with his boys two days a week and teaching them how to chip the ball by kicking it with the end of their foot above their big toe. He also looked forward to teaching them how to strike the ball underneath and how to dribble the ball with lots of little touches to keep the ball close. These skills were needed before the boys could begin to play soccer matches with each other.

He also was getting to know and like the boys on his team. He especially liked Miguel, who was eager to learn and tried very hard to perfect his skills. But at the same time, Miguel didn't hesitate to compliment a teammate if he performed well. Nicholas also couldn't help notice that there were two people who seemed to have a very special friendship with Miguel — one was Javier and the other was Pablo.

Chapter 14
Our Lady of Guadalupe

It was the middle of December and Nicholas was happy and adapting well to living and studying at Saint Juan Diego High School Seminary. He also was becoming a pretty good soccer coach, and he was well-liked and respected by the boys at the orphanage. Jose and he were close, like brothers, and now he had another person, Javier, who he was becoming good friends with.

The weather was perfect in the low 70s as Nicholas and Jose jogged through the courtyard for their weekly meeting with Father Reynolds. After all, they had to keep in shape since they were responsible for building the soccer teams at Holy Family Home.

"Well, gentlemen," Father Reynolds exclaimed as the boys approached him, "it appears that you are taking your responsibilities as soccer coaches seriously and keeping fit by jogging through this seminary's courtyard."

"Yes, Father," answered Jose. "All those young boys that I teach have a lot of energy, and I have to make sure that I can keep up with them."

"Yes," Nicholas agreed. "Jogging is good exercise and we might as well take advantage of this good weather when back home it probably is snowing."

"As you know, tomorrow is December 12 and you don't have classes because it is the feast day of Our Lady of Guadalupe. And you are quite right, Mr. Gilroy, we should take advantage of this good weather. That is why I have arranged for us to go on a pilgrimage to the Basilica of Our Lady of Guadalupe in Mexico City to attend Mass. Padre Ramirez has been very generous and is lending me his car for the trip. But since it is about a three-hour drive from here and I am not familiar with the roads, Mother Monica has offered to have Pablo be our guide and driver."

"Oh, Father Reynolds, thank you," Nicholas quickly responded with enthusiasm.

"Yes, thank you, Father," Jose happily responded.

"Since it will be a long trip, make sure you get up early enough to have breakfast before we leave. I will meet you in the foyer at 7:30."

Father Reynolds, Nicholas and Jose went over the events of the week, discussing any questions or concerns they may have had. The meeting came to an end after the three of them prayed Our Lady's Rosary together.

As Nicholas and Jose walked back to their dorm room, they were full of excitement and anticipation about their trip to the biggest religious celebration in the country of Mexico to honor the Blessed Mother. Nicholas felt in his heart that this pilgrimage was a great blessing and that it would bring him even closer to Our Lady.

The next morning when Father Reynolds and the boys arrived at Holy Family Home, Pablo was waiting in front of the chapel for them.

"Buenos dias," greeted Pablo.

"Buenos dias," Father Reynolds, Nicholas and Jose all responded joyfully.

Handing the car keys to Pablo, Father Reynolds said, "Thank you, Pablo, for taking us to Mexico City so that we can celebrate this wonderful feast day of Our Lady of Guadalupe."

"Amigos, you help Mother Monica and all the boys here and so, I help you."

With Pablo behind the wheel, Father Reynolds, Nicholas and Jose could relax and enjoy the Mexican countryside. Each one also could spend time in silent prayer and in contemplating how blessed they were to be able to attend Mass where Our Lady appeared to Saint Juan Diego.

They had been riding for a while when Father Reynolds broke the silence. "Let's pray the Rosary. Since this is the feast day of Our Lady of Guadalupe, it would be appropriate to pray the five Joyful Mysteries — The Annunciation, The Visitation, The Nativity, The Presentation and The Finding of Our Lord in the Temple."

Although he didn't participate, Pablo couldn't help sense the love and devotion that this priest and these two seminarians had for Our Lady of Guadalupe.

Upon entering Mexico City, it was obvious to everyone why Mother Monica had suggested that Pablo drive and be their guide. Mexico City was big with many buildings and people, and the roads were bumper to bumper with cars.

Pablo, sounding like a tour guide, said, "Mexico City is the largest city in the Western Hemisphere and it has a population of over twenty-one million people. Like your Washington, D.C., is the capital of your country, Mexico City is the capital of my country."

As they got closer to the shrine, there were thousands of people on bicycles or walking, and there were many families with children who were dressed in traditional Mexican costumes. Even some of the trucks, cars and bicycles were gaily decorated. Many of the people who were walking were carrying pictures of Our Lady of Guadalupe. Father Reynolds and the two seminarians were humbled and greatly inspired to see the powerful faith and love that the Mexican people openly displayed for the Mother of God.

Pablo, surprised to see so many people, exclaimed, "Amigos, are all these people going to the church?"

"Yes," responded Father Reynolds. "Padre Ramirez told me that almost two million people from all over Mexico come on this feast day of Our Lady of Guadalupe to attend Mass, which is celebrated every hour today. He told me that thousands of people travel many days just to be here."

Shaking his head, Pablo said, "I don't understand why so many make this journey."

Nicholas, so concerned about Pablo's lack of faith, didn't hesitate to say, "Oh, Pablo, the people come because they love Our Lady of Guadalupe and they know that she loves them. Some come to ask Our Lady for her help and protection, and some come to thank her for what she has done for them."

Without saying another word, Pablo again just shook his head in disbelief.

Pablo was able to park the car in one of the big parking lots, and the four of them joined the great multitude of people that were walking toward the Basilica. Pablo, Nicholas and Jose were very surprised to see hundreds of pilgrims making their way on their knees.

Father Reynolds, sensing their amazement, said, "These people are on their knees because it is a sign of their devotion and gratitude to Our Lady for a favor that they have received from her intercession. Like the shrines of Lourdes and Fatima, this, too, is a place of miracles."

Nicholas could feel the warmth and great spiritual devotion of the Mexican people as he walked beside them. He also could feel the love that they had for the Mother of God. *If only Pablo could feel your love, Mary,* prayed Nicholas.

The Basilica of Our Lady of Guadalupe was immense. It was circular in design with seven doors that represented the seven gates of celestial Jerusalem referred to by Jesus. It could accommodate up to ten thousand people for the celebration of Mass.

Because of the circular floor plan, no matter where people were in the church, it was possible for everyone to see Saint Juan Diego's tilma with the miraculous image of Our Lady of Guadalupe on it. For protection, it was encased in bullet-proof glass above the altar. There were nine chapels on the main floor. Under the main floor there were ten more chapels, and the basilica's crypts with fifteen thousand niches.

Before they could go inside, Pablo stopped and said, "Amigos, you go ahead. I will stay here and wait for you."

Nicholas, greatly concerned about Pablo's lack of faith, quickly responded, "But Pablo, we want you to come with us."

Father Reynolds, in a tone that rang with authority and wisdom, said, "We don't want Pablo to feel uncomfortable. He need not come with us. Pablo, we will meet you after Mass on Tepeyac Hill, which is right over there. They say that it is very beautiful with trees and flowers. It will be a very good place for you to sit and rest before your long drive back to the seminary."

Before Pablo could respond, Father Reynolds continued, "Now gentlemen, let's go inside before Mass begins."

Pablo watched Father Reynolds, Nicholas and Jose disappear behind one of the seven doors and, turning his head, he looked up at Tepeyac Hill. Pausing for a moment, he did what Father Reynolds had suggested and began to ascend the stone steps to the top of the hill.

The winding pilgrim's path was terraced and bordered by flowering shrubs, manicured lawns and many waterfalls that cascaded down the hillside. At the top of the hill were lush gardens of flowers, especially roses, and a small chapel. On both sides of the chapel were two huge marble angels. The inscriptions on the statues indicated that one was the Archangel Michael and the other was the Archangel

Gabriel, and they seemed to be guarding the little chapel.

Looking up at the impressive and mighty statue of the Archangel Michael, a strong feeling came over Pablo. His whole being sensed that he was on holy ground and that he needed to go into the chapel. Walking toward the door, Pablo paused and thought, *Do I dare enter this sacred place*, and then he slowly went inside.

Pablo's eyes were immediately drawn to the picture of Our Lady of Guadalupe in a golden frame above the simple altar. His whole being felt that he truly was in the presence of a holy queen so he bowed, and then he fell to his knees.

When Mass was over, Father Reynolds, Nicholas and Jose made their way up the stone stairs to the top of the Hill of Tepeyac. Not finding Pablo outside, they went inside the chapel. All three of them were taken by surprise to see Pablo kneeling. Father Reynolds must have been divinely inspired because he told Nicholas and Jose to wait outside and then he approached Pablo.

Nicholas and Jose didn't mind spending time in the lush garden with the two impressive marble archangels. It gave them time to reflect on the events of this important feast day of Our Lady of Guadalupe. Moreover, they realized that whatever had happened to Pablo, he needed the spiritual guidance of Father Stephen Reynolds.

Chapter 15
Feliz Navidad

Christmas Mass was always very special for Nicholas. He truly believed that the celebration of the birth of Jesus and the idea that God would become a human being was a profound reality to be pondered and cherished.

This Christmas was going to be different because it would be the first time that he would not be with his family. However, what kept him from feeling sad was the fact that he would be with Father Reynolds and Jose. They were going to Holy Family Home where Father Reynolds would be celebrating Mass, and then they would be staying to enjoy a Christmas meal with the Sisters, all the orphaned boys and Pablo.

Another reason that Nicholas was not sad was the fact that, thanks to Javier, they were bringing Christmas gifts to all the boys. Javier had convinced his father, Señor Santiago, to buy the boys soccer uniforms, soccer cleats, socks, shin guards, soccer balls and two new goal frames. For the boys who were too young to play, he had bought books and toys.

To be with Mother Teresa's Sisters, who, like him, were also far from home, and the orphaned boys made Nicholas realize the special nature of this Christmas. Christ came into the world in a simple way and not in a grand or mighty way. He came into the world in a humble way with a manger for his bed.

Father Reynolds had spent the day before at Holy Family hearing the confessions of the boys. He was convinced that the boys were being influenced by Nicholas and Jose, who they greatly admired for helping them with English, in coaching them in soccer, and for following their calling to be Catholic priests. Father Reynolds was certain that there were a few boys at the orphanage who had that same calling.

Before the beginning of Mass, under the direction of Sister Mary Claire, their music teacher, the boys in the choir sang Christmas carols in praise of God on this most holy day. The boys, ranging in age from ten to seventeen, were dressed in simple white robes that were handmade by the Sisters and some of the women in town. When the medley of songs finished, the lead tenor, a boy by the name of Esteban, with a voice like an angel, began to sing "Silent Night."

As soon as Esteban finished singing, the Mass began. A small boy by the name of Felipe led the procession and carried the censor with incense. The strong aroma that filled the chapel reminded everyone that something sacred was about to take place. Right behind Felipe were Nicholas and Jose as the altar servers dressed in their cassock and surplice, followed by Father Reynolds.

The Mass proceeded as usual. When it came time for the readings, two boys from the orphanage stepped forward. When they had finished, the choir sang the Psalm and Hallelujah. Father Reynolds then stepped forward to proclaim the Gospel of Saint Luke.

"In those days a decree went out from Caesar Augustus that the whole world should be enrolled. This was the first enrollment, when Quirinius was governor of Syria. So, all went to be enrolled, each to his own town. And Joseph, too, went from Galilee from the town of Nazareth to Judea, to the city of David that is called Bethlehem, because he was of the house and family of David, to be enrolled with Mary, his betrothed, who was with child. While they were there, the time came for her to have her child, and she gave birth to her firstborn son. She wrapped him in swaddling clothes and laid him in a manger because there was no room for them in the inn.

"Now there were shepherds in that region living in the fields and keeping the night watch over their flock. The angel of the Lord appeared to them and the glory of the Lord shone around them, and they were struck with great fear. The angel said to them, *'Do not be afraid; for behold, I proclaim to you good news of great joy that will be for all the people. For today in the city of David a savior has been born for you who is Christ and Lord. And this will be a sign for you: you will find an infant wrapped in swaddling clothes and lying in a manger.'* And suddenly there was a multitude of the heavenly host with the angel, praising God and saying: *'Glory to God in the highest and on earth peace to those on whom his favor rests.'* The Gospel of the Lord."

Pausing, Father Reynolds began his homily. "Two brothers, ages six and eight, were always getting into trouble. Their mother found out that the priest in her parish was very successful in disciplining children, so she asked him if he would speak to her boys. The priest agreed to speak to them. However, he asked to see them individually. The eight-year-old went in first while his mother and younger brother waited outside the priest's office. The priest, a huge man with a deep booming voice, sat the boy down and asked him sternly, *'Do you know where God is, son?'* Thinking that the boy might say God is everywhere or God is in our hearts, the boy made no response and just sat there wide-eyed with his mouth hanging open. Now the priest repeated the question in an even sterner tone, *'Where is God?'* Again, the boy made no attempt to answer. Finally, the priest raised his voice even more and shook his finger in the boy's face and bellowed, *'Where is God?'* The boy screamed and bolted from the room, grabbed his younger brother by the hand and ran directly home, up the stairs to their bedroom and slammed the door. When the younger brother asked, *'What happened?'* The older brother, gasping for breath, replied, *'We are in BIG trouble this time. GOD is missing and they think We did it!'*

Waiting a moment for the laughter to die down, Father Reynolds continued his homily. "Is God missing from our lives? Christmas is a time when God comes into the world and into our lives in a special way. He comes as the Christ child born in that lowly manger. Jesus Christ wants to be at the very center of our lives. What is required of us is obedience and trust that what God wants for us is the very best. What is required of us is gratitude. To be grateful for all that we have. What is required of us is generosity, to be people that give and help those in need.

"Remember the words of the angel, *'Do not be afraid; for behold, I proclaim to you good news of great joy that will be for all the people. For today in the city of David a savior has been born for you who is Christ and Lord. And this will be a sign for you: you will find an infant wrapped in swaddling clothes and lying in a manger.'* And suddenly there was a multitude of the heavenly host with the angel, praising God and saying: *'Glory to God in the highest and on earth peace to those on whom his favor rests.'*

"Christmas is a time for giving gifts. At every Mass a great miracle takes place. The bread and wine become the Body and Blood of Jesus Christ, the best gift anyone could ever receive."

Nicholas thought about the powerful words of Father Reynolds and the great miracle that happens at every Mass. He also pondered the role of angels who are sent to us as messengers from God, as our spiritual guides, and as our helpers in times of danger. He knew first hand that angels are real and that everyone has a guardian angel. For when he was in great danger an angel by the name of Raphael was sent to help him. He then silently prayed: *Angel of God, my guardian dear, to whom God's love commits me here, ever this day, be at my side, to light and guard, to rule and guide.*

Chapter 16

The Feast of the Three Kings

Because all the boys were on Christmas break, Saint Juan Diego High School Seminary became a quiet and peaceful place. Father Reynolds used this time as an opportunity to give the boys a mini-retreat. The day after Christmas, he had them begin a Novena to Our Lady of Guadalupe to ask her for an increase in vocations to the priesthood and religious life, and for her to protect and guide all the seminarians at Saint Juan Diego and at Saint Peter's back home.

During those nine days of prayers to Our Lady, they went to the chapel where Father Reynolds would then expose the Blessed Sacrament. The three of them would pray the Rosary, and after a period of silent Eucharistic Adoration, Father Reynolds would end with Benediction. Every day Father Reynolds also would celebrate Mass either at the seminary or at Holy Family Home for Mother Monica, her Sisters and all their boys. Nicholas and Jose were the altar servers, and, dressed in their cassock and surplice, they had a positive effect on all the boys, especially those who felt that God might be calling them also to the priesthood.

Nicholas and Jose were surprised and excited when Father Reynolds told them that Señor Santiago had invited them, along with Miguel, to his home on January 6 to celebrate Los Reyes Magos — the Feast of the Three Kings.

The boys were looking forward to seeing Javier, who had become their good friend. They also were happy that Miguel had been invited because it was obvious to them that Javier and the little orphan boy had a special friendship.

The Santiagos' home was about a thirty-minute drive from the seminary. The Spanish-style colonial mansion was made of white stucco and had a red tile roof. The intricate Spanish Renaissance ornamental spiral columns around every door and window were very impressive. Situated on one hundred acres of land, there was a large fenced off swimming pool with a thatched pagoda and a stable with six thoroughbred horses.

Javier had been anxiously waiting for his friends. The moment he saw their car approach the circular driveway, he ran out of his house to greet them with his three young sisters trailing behind him. Father Reynolds had barely come to a stop when Nicholas and Jose, taking Miguel by the hand, bolted out of the car.

"Quite the little homestead," Jose said jokingly.

"And I see that you have many horses. I think, Amigo, that maybe you might be a Mexican cowboy in disguise," Nicholas chimed in.

"Now I know why I missed you guys," Javier said with a laugh. "You keep me humble." Giving Miguel a hug, Javier continued, "And I missed you, too, my little friend."

Miguel, overwhelmed by the lavish surroundings, was lost for words and he could only nod his head.

Now conscious of his three siblings, who were giggling, Javier said, "Nicholas, Jose and Miguel, I want you to meet my sisters: Maria is eight, Francisca is eleven and Josefina is fourteen. So, you see, I truly am their big brother."

But before either Nicholas or Jose could say another word, all eyes were on Señor Ricardo Santiago and his wife as they made their way outside to greet their guests.

"Welcome, Padre Reynolds. This is my wife, Christina. And this must be Nicholas, Jose and

Miguel. My son has told me so much about all of you. Welcome!"

"Thank you, Señor and Señora Santiago for inviting us to your home," replied Father Reynolds.

"Padre, please call us Ricardo and Christina. I have planned a special celebration for all of you on this Feast of the Three Kings. Now let's go inside and talk for a while before we eat. Javier and girls, why don't you take the boys for a tour of our land?"

The spacious living room of this elegant home had floor-to-ceiling French doors with a tranquil view of a ceramic tile patio surrounded by a garden with beautiful flowers and trees. Since Mrs. Santiago had help who prepared and cooked the meals, she was able to join her husband and Father Reynolds in the living room.

"Señor Ricardo, it is obvious that you have been very successful and that you have been able to provide your family with many things. God has been very generous to you."

"Padre, I owe my success to my ancestors and to my keen ability to do business and not to God. For you see, my ancestors were one of the original families that came here from Spain and invested in the silver mines.

As one of the major shareholders, I have used some of this money to start a company that makes flat screens for televisions and computer monitors."

"Yes, you have been very successful, but still it is God who has allowed all of this to have happened to you," Father Reynolds responded.

"Maybe this is so, but that doesn't give God the right to think that I should give Him my son. All Javier talks about are your Nicholas and Jose and how wonderful that they are going to be Catholic priests. So, make sure that you don't encourage him with foolish ideas about becoming a priest, like you."

"A priest like me?" Father Reynolds asked.

"Señor Ricardo smiled. "Por favor, Padre, no offense is intended. We need priests, of course, just not my son. He has other responsibilities to his family. His family must come first."

"A vocation to the priesthood is a gift from God," Father Reynolds responded. "It is not a simple career choice. If your son is given that gift, it is to be cherished and celebrated, not dismissed."

"Padre, we will have to agree to disagree. You must understand, that a man in my position has many responsibilities. Romantic notions of my son becoming a priest are not acceptable. There are plenty of others, like your Nicholas and your Jose. They will be good priests, I am sure."

"Ricardo," Christina interrupted, "have you grown so distant from God? Do you not remember the promise you made when Javier was born?"

"Now, let's not bore the good Padre with that . . ."

Christina continued. "When Javier was born, he was not well, and he was not breathing properly. He was close to death. I remember the prayer Ricardo made at my bedside with our baby in my arms. He knelt down and pleaded with God that if Javier got better, he promised that he would give our son to Him. And he asked Our Lady of Guadalupe, Saint Juan Diego and Saint Jose Sanchez del Rio for their help. God was generous and gave our son life. My husband forgets the promise he made to God, but God does not forget."

"I have been very generous to the Church. And I will continue to be generous, but not the life of my son to be a priest. Not that!" said Señor Ricardo in a defiant tone.

All conversation ended when they heard the happy voices of the Santiago children and their guests as they entered the house. They came in just in time for Carmen, the cook, to tell everyone that dinner was ready.

The Santiagos' dining room also was elegantly decorated with Baroque-style furniture. The dining room table and chairs were made from white oak and had intricate hand carvings. The ornate chairs were upholstered with material that was a combination of leather and fabric. Like the living room, the dining room had a wall of French doors so that one could see and enjoy the beautiful garden of flowers and trees.

Señor Ricardo Santiago was very proud of his Spanish heritage. He wanted Father Reynolds, Nicholas and Jose, because they were from the United States to experience a typical Spanish style Christmas meal. But at the same time, he wanted them to experience the Mexican tradition of the Feast of the Three Kings.

When everyone was seated, Señor Santiago turned to Father Reynolds and said, "Padre, would you do us the honor by saying a prayer before we eat."

"Almighty God, we give you thanks for the food we are about to receive. We pray for all those who are hungry and without adequate food. Please help them

Heavenly Father and make us instrumental in helping all who are poor and in need. We ask all this through Christ, Our Lord. Amen."

The first thing that Carmen brought out to eat were cheese puffs, drizzled with honey on top. A Spanish seafood soup with plenty of shrimp came next. Then came the main course, which consisted of roast lamb, potatoes lightly fried in extra virgin oil, and white asparagus with oil and vinegar.

When everyone had finished eating Señor Santiago said, "Today, the Feast of the Three Wise Men, is very special for both the people of Spain and Mexico. We celebrate that the three kings brought the gifts of gold, frankincense and myrrh to the Baby Jesus by the baking of a special cake. And baked inside this special cake is a little figurine of the Baby Jesus."

Now Carmen brought out a large sweet bread cake with candied fruit on top shaped in the form of a wreath. Called *rosca de reyes,* which means *kings' wreath,* it represented the crowns worn by the three kings. As Carmen cut pieces of cake, she placed it on the dish in front of each person. When she came to Miguel and cut his piece, the figurine of Baby Jesus was inside and everyone clapped.

Miguel, with a look of surprise, could only say, "Wow!"

"Well, Miguel," Señor Santiago said, smiling, "it looks like you are the one who will have good luck this year. And because it is the tradition that you also have to have a tamales party on Candlemas Day, February 2, and invite all of us, I will help you do this. We will all meet again at Holy Family, and I will provide all the food for us and for all the boys and the Sisters, too."

Now it was Father Reynolds who responded. "Thank you, Señor Ricardo for your generous offer. I am sure that Mother Monica and her Sisters and the boys at Holy Family will be very grateful. I know that they are very thankful to you for all the soccer uniforms and equipment that you have given their boys for Christmas.

"Nicholas, Jose and your son, Javier, have been working very hard coaching the boys, who have become pretty good soccer players. But they only play against each other. I have a request for you. You are well-known in San Miguel de Allende. Would it be possible for you to arrange a soccer game on February 2 between the boys at Holy Family and the boys from another school? And if Holy Family wins, then we will have something to celebrate."

"Padre, you are very wise. When it comes to my son, Javier, and his love of soccer, and all the time and effort he has put in to help these boys, how could I not say yes to your request."

Chapter 17
The Soccer Game

February 2, Candlemas Day, or the feast of the Presentation of Our Lord, celebrates the occasion when Mary and Joseph brought Jesus to the temple in Jerusalem forty days after his birth. This was done to fulfill the rite of purification of the mother. They also went to the temple to fulfill the law of Moses that said that every first-born male was to be consecrated to God. And according to the law, they were obliged to offer a sacrifice to God. Because Mary and Joseph were poor, they made an offering of two turtledoves.

In Mexico, Candlemas Day is celebrated because it reminds the people that as a baby they were presented to God in the Church by their parents through baptism. Unfortunately, in the United States this feast day has been replaced with the secular Groundhog Day.

This Candlemas Day was perfect weather for a soccer game. Señor Santiago was true to his word. He was able to arrange a soccer match between the boys at Holy Family Home and the boys at Saint Sabastian

High School, one of the Catholic high schools in San Miguel de Allende.

The atmosphere was charged with excitement because the boys at Holy Family were finally going to play against another high school soccer team. All the Sisters and all the other boys, along with Pablo and Señor Santiago, were eagerly awaiting the start of the game. Miguel's happiness and laughter for his tamales party after the game was uplifting and noticed by everyone.

The orphan boys had a feeling of confidence because of the new, green soccer uniforms they were wearing with *Holy Family Soccer Team* printed in big, black letters on the back of their shirts. They also had on their new soccer cleats, socks and shin guards. They stood tall and gave the boys from Saint Sabastian a determined look that could only mean they were going to win. Besides, they had complete trust in their coach, Javier, and his two assistants, Nicholas and Jose, that what they had taught them would make this win possible.

Before the two teams took to the field, Father Reynolds stood before them and said, "In the Name of the Father and of the Son and of the Holy Spirit.

Almighty God bless the boys on both teams as we begin our game. Help and protect them, not only in this soccer game, but in every aspect of their lives. And we ask the powerful intercession of Our Lady of Guadalupe to help and guide them to be young men of virtue and faith. Amen."

Now the two seniors who were captains of their soccer team stepped forward. Nicholas, before he tossed the coin to see which team would kick off first, turned to Fernando, the captain of Holy Family, and said, "Fernando, your call."

"Heads," replied Fernando.

With a flick of his wrist, Nicholas tossed the coin in the air and it landed "tails up."

Both teams took their places on the field. As soon as the whistle sounded the boys from Saint Sabastian began to kick the ball, passing well around the boys from Holy Family and down the field with a strong shot at the goal. But it was skillfully deflected away by Pedro the goalie from Holy Family.

Cheers rang out from the Sisters, their boys, Pablo, Señor Santiago, Jose and Nicholas. Only Javier, his eyes glued on every move made by both teams, didn't share in the cheering. He was too focused on how he was going to guide his team to victory. This small victory was short-lived because Saint Sabastian quickly regained control of the ball and shot it again and again, and on the third shot scored.

Jose shouted, "Lucky shot!" Then he turned to Nicholas and said, "We need some divine help, otherwise this game will soon be over and we are going to lose." So, Nicholas reached into his pocket and took his rosary beads out. He then silently prayed for God and Our Lady's help.

The soccer ball went back and forth and up and down the field. Fernando got control of the ball and kicked it down the field toward Saint Sabastian's net. Nicholas continued to pray even though everyone around him was shouting for joy. Watching from the side, Father Reynolds saw Nicholas with his rosary beads and smiled. Following the good example of his young high school seminarian, Father Reynolds took out his rosary beads and began silently praying, too.

Fernando paused, extended his leg and kicked the soccer ball with all the strength that he had. It sailed through the air and curved past Saint Sabastian's defenders and goalie. It was a goal, and everyone from Holy Family cheered and jumped up and down.

Nicholas heard someone yell, "Goal!" When he looked up to see who yelled out, for a split second he thought he saw Raphael. But when Nicholas blinked, he was gone.

The two teams were engaged in quite a battle and the tension was growing. First, the boys from Holy Family were in control of the ball. Then in a flash, the boys from Saint Sabastian had possession and were in control of the ball. By this time, Javier, Jose and many of the Sisters also were praying on their rosary beads.

Finally, the tide began to turn in favor of the orphan boys when Fernando got control of the ball and began kicking it down the field. Stopping just long enough, he gave the ball a swift kick and it sailed through the air and went right into Saint Sabastian's net, making the final winning goal score.

Everyone from Holy Family was cheering. Mother Monica, her Sisters and all their boys ran onto the field to hug their soccer players. Among all the excitement and jubilation and without anyone noticing, Nicholas fell to his knees and thanked God and Our Blessed Mother for their wonderous help.

Chapter 18

Saint Jose Sanchez del Rio

Father Reynolds knew how much Nicholas and Jose wanted to travel to the shrine of Saint Jose Sanchez del Rio before they left Mexico. It was the beginning of spring vacation and two weeks away from Holy Week. Father Reynolds felt that this would be the best time for the boys to go on this pilgrimage, so he arranged with Mother Monica to have Pablo be their guide and drive them. Since Javier had become a good friend to both Nicholas and Jose, Father Reynolds extended the invitation to him, too.

The sun was bright and high in the sky as the old Land Rover made its way along the road that led to Sahuayo and the Catholic Church of Saint James the Apostle. Nicholas and Jose were seated in the back, and Javier was up front with Pablo.

The dusty and tired SUV had seen many miles. Dark blue in color with many scratches, it was a reliable vehicle and served well the Sisters of the Missionaries of Charity. Pablo, its guardian and chief mechanic, had kept the Land Rover working well for years. He affectionately called the vehicle "milagro coche" (miracle car), as it was a miracle that it was still running after so many years of service.

"Amigos, how is the ride so far?" Pablo asked. "I know she is old but still, she is a good coche."

"Doing fine," Jose answered. "Thanks again for taking us, Pablo. We are excited to see the place where my namesake died and is buried."

"Amigos, you will see that it is a beautiful place filled with God's peace and grace."

"I have a question," said Javier. "I know that Jose Sanchez del Rio is a saint, but how does a person become a saint?"

"We studied this with Sister Mary Catherine," Nicholas exclaimed. "She called it the five-step process. Step One: The person normally has to be dead for at least five years before the local bishop begins his investigation to see if that person has lived a life of holiness or was martyred for the Church.

"Step Two: All this information is sent to the Congregation for the Cause for Saints in Rome.

"Step Three: If the cause for sainthood for that person is accepted by the Congregation, they then will begin their own investigation. If the person is approved by the Congregation, it goes before the Pope. If the Pope decides that the person lived a life of 'heroic virtue' that person can then be called Venerable.

"Step Four: A miracle needs to be attributed to prayers made to that person or that person has to have been martyred for the Church.

"Step Five: A second miracle needs to be attributed to prayers made to this person to be declared a saint. Martyrs, however, only need one verified miracle to become a saint."

"Oh, so that means that Jose Sanchez del Rio was a martyr, and he actually was responsible for a miracle, too," Javier exclaimed in astonishment.

Now it was Jose, with a big grin on his face, who responded. "I have to confess that when I found out that we were going on this pilgrimage, I went on the internet to learn more about Saint Jose, since he is my namesake."

Jose continued, "Saint Jose is credited with a miracle for a baby girl by the name of Lupis. Due to complications at birth, Lupis contracted meningitis and had epileptic seizures. Although she was put in a coma to help her condition, her mother was told that 90 percent of her brain had been damaged.

"Just as the doctors were going to take her off of life support, her mother asked if she could hold her. Because she was a woman of great faith, she prayed to Jose Sanchez del Rio to intervene to God, for she needed a miracle to save her child.

"Suddenly, baby Lupis opened her eyes and smiled and then laughed. The doctors were shocked and couldn't explain what had just happened. The doctors took more tests and scans which showed that the baby's brain had recovered and appeared to be normal."

"Lupis's mother knew that it was a miracle and that Jose Sanchez del Rio was responsible for that miracle," Nicholas added. "And that miracle was recognized by the Vatican and he was declared a saint."

"Wonderful! What a beautiful Church!" Pablo yelled. "And I know miracles happen, Amigos. I know from my own life."

After driving more than three hours, Pablo finally reached Sahuayo. He found a spot to park his beloved 'coche' and led the boys to Saint James the Apostle Church. Nicholas felt a surge of excitement and joy that he was finally going to see the place where Saint

Jose Sanchez del Rio was buried. The church was impressive with many beautiful flowers and shrubs growing throughout the grounds.

Leaving the warm sunlight, the four opened the heavy wooden door and entered the church. They found the temperature was much cooler inside. A large font of water was waiting for them to bless themselves. Passing through the vestibule, they entered the main part of the church, which was filled with simple wooden pews.

The eyes of the boys and Pablo were immediately drawn to the large marble ornate side altar dedicated to Saint Jose. In the center and above the altar in a golden frame was a large picture of Saint Jose. Two large reliquaries that contained the remains of the boy saint were on either side of the picture. Below and in front of the altar was a reclining wax figure of the young martyr encased in glass.

Nicholas was struck by how familiar he looked; not like a saint in a stained-glass window, but like a young man like himself, right down to his shirt and blue jeans.

Jose verbalized what Nicholas was thinking by saying, "He looks just like us. He could be one of our friends at the seminary."

Nicholas responded, "The great part is that he is one of our friends. He just happens to be in heaven."

Javier observed, "He seems so familiar to me, too, like an old friend. Like someone I might know from my high school, or from San Miguel de Allende, or even from the orphanage."

"That's one of the reasons Saint Jose is a great saint. He reminds us that he is no different than us. He had all the flaws we have. But he gave his heart to Jesus Christ, and it is Christ that can work through anyone to bring glory to God. Even the most common and ordinary person can become a saint." Nicholas continued, "All we need to do is to be humble and to be obedient to God."

With a sigh, Pablo said, "So beautiful and innocent. I wish I could be a saint someday."

"You can be," Nicholas quickly responded. "Every person is made in God's image and likeness, and can become a saint."

In a voice full of sadness, Pablo said, "Oh no, my friend, not me. I have done too much in my life to displease God."

Nicholas, with a heart full of compassion for Pablo, said, "To quote one of our teachers at Saint Peter's, Sister Mary Catherine, *'Every saint has a past and every sinner has a future.'* God can work miracles in our lives if we let Him. No one is beyond His mercy and redemption."

Nicholas's words struck Javier deeply. "Nicholas, do you think that even I could be what God wants me to be and not what my father wants?"

"God is your Father. But if you mean your Dad, then I think, Javier, that you need to listen to what God is calling you to do and follow and obey God first. Saint Joan of Arc often said that God must be served first."

Before they left the church, Pablo and the young men in his care prayed Our Lady's Rosary before the Blessed Sacrament in the tabernacle.

Once outside they walked to the town cemetery where Saint Jose was martyred. Surrounded by a garden of roses, flowering plants, shrubs and trees was the bronze figure of Saint Jose lying on the spot where he was killed. Behind him, engraved on a stone, were his words, *"Never has it been so easy to gain heaven."* And in bold letters around his bronze figure were Saint Jose's last words before he died, *"Viva Christo Rey."*

Nicholas asked Saint Jose to pray for him so that he would be able to do God's Will each day. He also asked Saint Jose to help him have the courage to never deny Jesus, even if it meant giving up his life and crying out like he did, *"Viva Christo Rey, Long live Christ the King."*

Chapter 19
Danger on the Highway

Before they left the city of Sahuayo for the trip back to San Miguel de Allende, Pablo took the boys to a little park next to Saint James the Apostle Church. Since they were hungry, the boys didn't waste any time in devouring the fried shredded beef empanadas and Mexican brownies that the seminary's cook had prepared for them. All were extremely glad that they each had a big thermos of cold water to quench their thirst.

As the "milagro coche," the car of miracles, rumbled along the hot and dusty road, Nicholas's thoughts were on Saint Jose Sanchez del Rio. He was inspired to grow closer to Jesus Christ because of the courage of this young saint who gave up his life for Christ and he thought, *but would I have the courage to give up my life for Christ and shout 'Viva Christo Rey' like he did?*

Jose, glancing at Nicholas, asked, "A penny for your thoughts?"

"I was just thinking about your namesake, Saint Jose, and how he had the courage to stand up to those soldiers who had threatened to kill him because he would not renounce his faith in Jesus Christ. That is so powerful."

"Yes," Jose agreed. "Such a commitment requires a maturity of spirit, a trust in Jesus, and a trust that heaven is real and so much better than here. The way that the Church grew, especially in the early days, was by the witness of many martyrs."

Nicholas nodded. "That's true. All the apostles, except Saint John, were martyrs for the faith. They traveled everywhere, even to places that were hostile to the message of Jesus Christ, and they did so without hesitation or fear."

Javier, who was moved by the conversation of his two American friends, said, "When you know Jesus, you don't have to be afraid of anything, do you?"

Nicholas responded, "That's true Javier; but I know that I still have many fears, so I have more work to do."

Jose laughed and said, "Don't worry, Nicholas. One day you will reach my level of spiritual maturity. Until then, I will help guide you by my good example."

Nicholas gave Jose a light punch in his arm. "Starting with your example of humility, right?"

But before Jose had a chance to answer, there was a loud rumbling sound. The SUV began rocking and swaying from side to side.

Pablo shouted, "Make sure your seat belts are on. It feels like an earthquake."

As the road in front of their "milagro coche" began to heave and split, Pablo quickly swerved to avoid a huge chasm that had been ripped wide open in what was once the highway.

Despite all the talk and good thoughts about courage, Nicholas knew that they were in serious trouble and he was overcome with fear. Pulling his rosary beads out of his pocket, he began to pray, asking Our Blessed Mother for her help and protection as the shaking of the ground and the swaying of the SUV increased.

There was a loud thunder-like sound, and rocks and earth began sliding down the hillside. Pablo and the boys were being shaken like cans of paint being mixed in a machine. The shaking now became even more violent. The SUV began to spin and was propelled into the air. It then bounced and jumped forward on the heaving pavement. Suddenly the SUV shot up and over to the side of the road and began tumbling down and rolling side to side. The screams of the terrified three boys were drowned out by the terrible crashing sound of metal.

When Pablo cried out, "Amigos, don't worry," the fear that Nicholas, Jose and Javier felt was quenched and a sense of calm came over them.

To an outside observer, no one inside that SUV, which was completely totaled, should have survived. However, Pablo's words must have been truly inspired because they knew that a miracle had happened. Pablo and all three boys had felt the warm embrace of Our Lady as she wrapped her mantle of protection around them in that out-of-control vehicle.

Now there was only an eerie silence as Nicholas and his three companions tried to comprehend what had just happened to them. Although the earthquake had lasted only a couple of minutes, it had done tremendous damage to the surroundings and to the SUV.

Nicholas and Jose were able to unfasten their seat belts and were the first to scramble out of the damaged SUV with minor scrapes and bruises. Pablo then emerged, gently pulling Javier.

Pablo knew that he was responsible for the safety of the boys. To reassure them that they would be all right, he broke the silence with, "Amigos, didn't I tell you that my "milagro coche" is a miracle car."

His joshing was exactly what the boys needed to hear and Jose, quickly responded, "Yes, as it is a miracle that we are all alive."

Nicholas and Jose turned their attention to Javier. It was clear that Javier was hurt, and Pablo was trying to determine the extent of his injuries. When Pablo saw the unusual angle of Javier's right leg, he knew that Javier's injury was serious. But when he tried to move it, Javier cried out in pain.

In a calm and reassuring voice, Pablo said, "Javier, I will make sure the pain will not be so bad."

Pablo then told Nicholas and Jose to bring him some tree branches. With his pocket knife, he cut them to fit the length of Javier's broken leg. He then cut off part of the sleeve of his shirt.

It was clear to Nicholas that Pablo was having a difficult time, and, with great concern, he asked, "Pablo, are you all right?"

"My collarbone, maybe it's broken." But not wanting to worry the boys, he said, "Don't worry, I have had worse injuries, but you have to help me with Javier."

Carrying the tree branches, Pablo knelt next to Javier, along with Nicholas and Jose. He told the boys to each take one of Javier's hands and hold it tightly to help keep him still.

In a calm voice, Pablo said, "Javier, this will hurt, but then it will make you feel better."

Javier let out a cry of pain as Pablo straightened his twisted leg. Now Pablo quickly went to work tying the tree branches around the broken leg with the material cut from the sleeve of his shirt.

The splint made the pain in Javier's leg better and he said, "Thanks, Pablo. If only my smartphone wasn't damaged in the car crash, we could have called for help."

"Don't worry, Javier. I will get help."

Pablo knew that a broken leg was not something to trifle with and that he would need to find help for himself and the boys as soon as possible.

It was a unanimous decision that Jose would stay with Javier and the wrecked SUV, and that Nicholas would go with Pablo to look for help. Two of the thermoses were not destroyed and each was almost half full of water. So, Jose and Javier kept one and Nicholas and Pablo took the other. Before he left, Nicholas gave Javier and then Jose a big hug.

Pablo knew that the journey without a vehicle and walking on foot would be dangerous, especially since he was injured. So, he silently prayed to Our Lady of Guadalupe and asked her for her motherly help so that he could keep the boys safe.

Chapter 20
Pablo's Story

Nicholas followed Pablo as they made their way out of the gully by climbing up the embankment to what was once the highway. Both Nicholas and Pablo were shocked at what they saw. The pavement was like a jigsaw puzzle with huge pieces of asphalt scattered all over, revealing the earth underneath. Giant rocks and boulders were everywhere. A seismic fault line under the highway and adjacent to the hillside was the cause of the earthquake.

In desperation Nicholas cried out, "Pablo, where will we find help?"

In a calm voice, Pablo responded, "Amigo, we trust in the Lord. Yes! All is blocked except across the desert. So that is where Our Lord is leading us to find help."

It was early in the afternoon and still warm. Pablo knew that they must not waste any time and that they had to travel when it was still light. The desert can be a very dangerous place at night.

The journey ahead seemed daunting to Nicholas as he and Pablo began walking. *Why did this happen?*

Jose and I were not injured, so God must have a plan in using us to help Javier and Pablo, he thought.

Turning to Our Lady for comfort and protection, Nicholas took out his rosary beads and said, "Pablo, why don't we pray a Rosary asking Our Lady of Guadalupe for her help and protection along our journey."

"Yes, Nicholas, I have been already asking her and now we will ask her together."

Their chant-like *Hail Mary's* drifted like music all around them and brought a sense of peace and comfort to the two forlorn travelers. When they had finished their Rosary, they walked in silence.

Pablo came to a halt in his walking and said, "Amigo, let's sit and rest and take a small drink."

Because of the injury to Pablo's collarbone, Nicholas was carrying the thermos in his small backpack. They only drank enough to quench their thirst. Then, after resting for a few more minutes, they continued on their way.

"Nicholas, what is your family like?"

Without breaking his stride, Nicholas answered, "Well, I am the oldest. I turned sixteen in December. I have a sister, Elizabeth, who is thirteen. My mom is a homemaker and my dad is a history professor in a Catholic college. I was homeschooled and both my mom and dad were my teachers until I enrolled in the ninth grade at Saint Peter's High School Seminary because I feel that God is calling me to be a Catholic priest."

"Oh, amigo, you have been given a good family. Yes, and to be a Catholic priest is very special."

"Pablo, what is your family like?"

"Very different. I don't have any brothers or sisters. My mama died giving me life. My papa took me to his sister's home. I lived with her and her husband and five children. I didn't see my papa much. Only two or three times a year. He left everything and went to work in the silver mines when my mama died. Every month he would send my aunt money. This was payment for keeping me, and it was a great help to my aunt and her family."

"Pablo, it sounds like your dad tried the best he could to make sure you were taken care of."

"Yes, in the things of this world, but not spiritually. You see, Nicholas, when my mama died, he blamed God and turned away from Him. I was not to be baptized or taught anything about the Catholic

Church. So even though my aunt and uncle tried to live their Catholic faith, they also tried to do what my papa wanted and they made sure that I had nothing to do with the church. You see, the money he sent was very important.

"Then one day when I was eighteen, my papa came to get me so that I could work with him in the silver mines. Although it was hard work with many hours spent under the earth, I was happy being with my papa. I never worked extra hours, but my papa did. One day he stayed behind to work extra hours. I had just left when I heard a terrible sound and the mine collapsed. It took three days before they could reach the miners, but they were all dead. So now I lost my mama and my papa and I, too, blamed God."

Filled with compassion and sorrow, Nicholas grabbed Pablo's hands and both stopped in their tracks. "Oh, Pablo, you are not that person anymore. You help Mother Monica and all the boys at the orphanage and you love Jesus and Our Lady of Guadalupe."

Before Pablo could respond and finish his story, the ground began to shake again. This time the shaking was so sharp and quick it made Nicholas fall.

Tumbling down the embankment, he landed next to a stream of water. But before he could get up, he was confronted with a grave threat to his life — a huge diamondback rattlesnake! The tremor and Nicholas's fall had scared the snake. Frozen in fear, Nicholas's world moved almost in slow motion as he heard and saw the rattling of the tail and the coiled body of the snake ready to strike him.

In one quick movement Pablo sprung forward and fell to the ground. As Nicholas felt the strong arms of Pablo pushing him away from harm, he also heard Pablo cry out in pain. Instead of Nicholas, the snake bit Pablo and then it quickly slithered away. But the damage had been done.

Now it was Nicholas who rushed forward to come to Pablo's aid, and, with his voice shaking with emotion, said, "Oh Pablo, you saved my life from that snake and now you've been bitten."

Considering what had just happened and the danger that he was in, Pablo said in a calm voice, "Nicholas, I need your help. The snake bit me on my leg. Help me over to that big rock so I can sit against it."

Once there Pablo took out his pocket knife and began cutting his pants below his right knee. When Nicholas saw the two puncture wounds from the fangs of the rattlesnake and how the leg was beginning to bruise and swell, he cried out, "Pablo, you need help and I don't know what to do!"

"Nicholas, my amigo, don't be afraid. Before I tell you what you must do, I need to finish my story.

"After the death of my papa, I made up my mind to never again go back down in that terrible place of death. I began working and getting people for a *coyote*. That is what we call a person who smuggles people in my country across the border to your country to work illegally as farm laborers. Sometimes, I would get whole families to go. These people would give all the money that they had to the *coyote*. I didn't think it was bad. They would have a better life than me and my papa had working in the mines."

"Ten years ago, the trip across the desert was long and the day was very hot. When we stopped the truck to check on the people, they were dead. All eight of them, except for one little boy about a year old. The *coyote* turned the truck around and we headed back where we had started. I don't know what happened after that because I took the little boy.

"I had great sorrow and guilt. I had told these people that they would have a better life and now they were dead. I knew that I had to help this little boy. So, I took him to Holy Family Home, where the Sisters of Mother Teresa would take good care of him."

"Oh, that little boy is Miguel," exclaimed Nicholas.

"Yes, it is Miguel. I needed to make up for the bad that I had done, so I became the handyman and helper at the orphanage in exchange for a place to live and food to eat, taking very little money. I also wanted to be close to Miguel.

"Do you remember when I drove you, Jose and Father Reynolds to the Shrine of Our Lady of Guadalupe? I didn't go inside because I was unworthy of Holy Mass. And then Father Reynolds told me to go and wait on top of Tepeyac Hill.

"When I got to the top it was a beautiful place with so many flowers and I felt at peace. Then looking up at the statue of San Miguel the angel, I got a most powerful thought that I was in a very holy place and that I needed to go into the chapel.

"As soon as I entered, I saw the beautiful picture of Our Lady of Guadalupe. I bowed because I knew that she is a holy queen and the great Mother of God. Suddenly, I fell on my knees because I felt something. It is hard for me to put into words. I felt a madre's love, something I had never known. And then my heart felt great pain and sorrow and I cried out, *God, please forgive me for all the evil that I have done.*

"Then in the most loving and beautiful voice, Our Lady of Guadalupe spoke to me. Yes, the great and holy Mother of God spoke to me, a sinner. She said that God knew that I had great sorrow for what I had done. He knew that I had changed from my selfish ways. She said that God wanted me to know that I was loved and forgiven, but there was something that I had to do. She told me that God wanted me to be baptized and join the Church.

"I told all this to Padre Reynolds, who is a good and holy priest. For months he has been giving me instructions and preparing me to be baptized at the Easter Vigil. Nicholas, I can't go on. You will have to leave me and go for help. You must not think about me but think about Jose and Javier. I am not afraid to die, but I am so sorry that I can't be baptized like God wanted."

Kneeling next to Pablo, with tears streaming from his eyes, Nicholas said in a tender voice, "Pablo, you will do what God wants. I know what to do and I can and I will baptize you."

Pablo watched in amazement as Nicholas took his thermos and ran down to the small stream of water. With his thermos full of water, he ran back and knelt next to Pablo again.

Placing his hands in Pablo's, Nicholas said, "Pablo, after every one of my questions say, *I do*." In a voice trembling with emotion, Nicholas repeated the words that Father Reynolds had taught him in his Catechism class.

"Do you reject Satan?"

"I do."

"And all his works?"

"I do."

"And all his empty promises?"

"I do."

"Do you believe in God the Father, almighty, creator of heaven and earth?"

"I do."

"Do you believe in Jesus Christ, His only Son, Our Lord, who was born of the Virgin Mary, was crucified, died, and was buried, rose from the dead and is now seated at the right hand of the Father?"

"I do."

"Do you believe in the Holy Spirit, the Holy Catholic Church, the communion of saints, the forgiveness of sins, the Resurrection of the body and life everlasting?"

"I do."

"This is our faith. This is the faith of the Church. We are proud to profess it, in Christ, Jesus, Our Lord. Amen."

With tears still streaming from his eyes and feeling the grace of God and the steady hand of the Blessed Virgin Mary, Nicholas now let the water from the thermos trickle over Pablo's head as he said, *"I baptize you in the Name of the Father and of the Son and of the Holy Spirit. Amen."*

"Nicholas, now have I joined the Church?"

Taking Pablo's hands in his again, Nicholas said with great tenderness, "You not only have joined the Church, Pablo, you have become a new creation through the water and the Holy Spirit and all of your sins have been forgiven."

Now it was Pablo who had tears streaming from his eyes as he said, "My dear amigo, you have given me the greatest gift."

Chapter 21
Saving Nicholas

Pablo's joy lasted only a few minutes. In a very serious voice, he said, "Nicholas, you know I can't travel. The only chance that Jose, Javier and I have is for you to leave me here and go for help."

With his voice shaking, Nicholas responded, "Yes, Pablo, I know. But I don't know the way and I am so afraid."

"Yes, when you leave me, I, too, will be afraid. But we won't be alone. We must trust. Yes! We must trust that Our Lady of Guadalupe will send her angels to protect us and to guide you to find help. Go while it is still light and follow the stream of water in that direction," as he pointed the way.

Nicholas then took his rosary beads from his pocket and placed them in Pablo's hands. "Pablo, I have my Miraculous Medal around my neck for protection and you need protection, too. Take my rosary beads and while I am gone, pray to Our Lady."

"Yes, Nicholas, I will pray to Our Lady of Guadalupe that you are protected and that you will bring back help for me, Jose and Javier."

With tears in their eyes, they hugged each other. Slowly, Nicholas turned and began to walk down the embankment toward the stream of water.

But before he could continue, Nicholas suddenly stopped. He turned around and looked up at the man who had become his friend and had saved his life, and shouted, "Don't worry Pablo. Our Lady of Guadalupe will protect and take care of both of us." And then with a heavy heart and with great fear Nicholas began his solitary journey to find help.

Traveling across the barren and hostile desert, Nicholas turned to Our Lady and prayed her Rosary, using his fingers to mark off the *Our Fathers* and the *Hail Marys*. Sometimes he would say these prayers silently, and other times he would say them out loud, which made him feel that he wasn't alone. Meditating on the different mysteries for each decade helped him to concentrate on the life of Mary and her Son, Jesus Christ. And this brought Nicholas great spiritual strength and comfort.

As the sun began to descend in the sky, the temperature became cooler, and the light began to fade. Nicholas's world now looked very different. It was harder for him to see where he was going, and it was even harder for him to see what was lurking before him. And in the dark his imagination played tricks on him and made him think things were out there that were not. Nicholas was thankful for the small flashlight that he had in his backpack and he took it out.

A cool breeze brought a chill to Nicholas as he sensed something sinister. Suddenly, he heard a strange howl that sent shivers down his spine. In the semidarkness he could make out what appeared to be a pack of big dogs. But as the animals got closer, Nicholas knew instinctively that this was no pack of dogs. This was a pack of wolves and he counted seven of them.

Frozen in fear, Nicholas could feel his heart pounding in his chest. The light from his small flashlight enabled him to see that the dark, gray lead wolf with eerie, yellow eyes and bared teeth was slowing and aggressively moving towards him. It's terrifying deep and guttural growling sounds were baying the rest of the pack to follow.

Walking ever so slowly, Nicholas began to back up and thought, *I'm going to die*! Then instinct took over. Nicholas turned and ran. He was running faster and harder than he ever did in any of his football or soccer games. Barking at each other, the wolves ran and spread out around Nicholas as they got ready to make their attack.

Like a voice crying in the wilderness, Nicholas shouted, "Oh Mary, Mother of God, please save me!"

What happened next defied reason. Suddenly, someone with tremendous strength who he couldn't see but could feel was lifting him higher and higher.

He then heard a voice so beautiful say, "Do not be afraid. Do you not know that you are under my protection."

Nicholas's whole being was consumed with peace and great joy because he knew that the great Mother of God had just spoken to him.

And in a *blink of the eye,* Nicholas found himself lying facedown on the ground and far away from the pack of attacking wolves. Getting up from the ground, Nicholas expected to see Our Lady but was taken by surprise to see Raphael instead.

With a voice full of emotion and gratitude, Nicholas exclaimed, "Oh, Raphael you've saved my life again. And I now know that you are an angel. Are you my guardian angel?"

"Yes, Nicholas. I am your guardian angel. We Guardian angels are the servants of God. Our mission is to surround the person we are assigned to so that we can protect, guide and intercede to heaven for them. You have been given a great gift. Because I am a spirit, God has allowed me to take on a human form so that you can see me. Both times when you were in grave danger of dying Our Lady sent me to protect you. She has done this because she knows your heart. She knows that you have great love for her and her Son. You have shown this by the many Rosaries you pray to her, the Miraculous Medal that you wear and the many good things that you do for others. But most of all, it is because you have said, *Yes,* to God's call to be a Catholic priest. For you see, Nicholas, your life has been saved so that you can bring many souls to Jesus Christ."

Nicholas, speechless, was trying to comprehend what he had just heard, when Raphael continued. "Nicholas, we have to act quickly."

His guardian angel took Nicholas by the hand and, quick as a flash, they now were standing in the courtyard of a quaint Spanish- style house.

"The man who lives here is a good person and he will get you the help you need for Jose, Javier and Pablo."

As Nicholas looked at the house, he gave a big sigh of relief because he realized that his journey for help was finally over. He then turned to Raphael, but he was gone.

Chapter 22
Viva Christo Rey

Nicholas's sophomore year as an exchange student at Saint Juan Diego High School Seminary was coming to an end. He was thankful to God that he was able to spend this time living with the Mexican people and seeing how fervent they were in the practice of their Catholic faith, especially in their devotion to Our Lady of Guadalupe. He was thankful to God that he had been given the opportunity to help the Sisters of the Missionaries of Charity by coaching their boys in soccer, and he was thankful to God for the many friendships that he had made.

But most of all, he was thankful to God for the help and for the protection from Our Lady and his guardian angel when his life was in great danger. He realized that all the heartaches and challenges he had encountered happened for a reason, and he was more determined than ever to follow his vocation to be a Catholic priest.

It was the first week in June and a beautiful, sunny day as Father Reynolds drove Nicholas and Jose to Holy Family Home. Mother Monica wanted to see them before they left to go back home to the United States.

They rode in silence, for each one was absorbed in their thoughts and in the emotions they were feeling. The bond between Nicholas and Jose had grown even stronger during their time in Mexico. They both knew that God had used them in a special way to give comfort and spiritual help to someone in need. For Nicholas, it was Pablo, and for Jose, it was Javier.

As soon as the three of them got out of the car, Perrito ran up to be petted, while Mother Monica watched as she stood in front of the chapel .

"Bueno dias, Mother Monica."

"Bueno dias, Father Reynolds," Mother Monica said with a big smile. "You know that I couldn't let you leave Mexico without thanking all of you for everything that you have done here at Holy Family Home to help us with our boys. Now, we don't have time to waste, so please come with me."

Mother Monica walked quickly, and Father Reynolds, Nicholas and Jose followed her stride toward the building that served as the kitchen and dining hall for the orphanage. As soon as Mother Monica opened the door a chorus of happy voices cried out, *"Viva Christo Rey! Long Live Christ the King!"*

Father Reynolds, Nicholas and Jose were so surprised that they were speechless. The Sisters of the Missionairies of Charity, all the boys of Holy Family Home, some dressed in their soccer uniforms, Señor Ricardo Santiago, Javier, and Pablo, sitting in a wheelchair, were all there to greet them. The dining hall was decorated with a big banner that read *Viva Christo Rey, Long Live Christ the King,* and a large statue of Saint Jose Sanchez del Rio was on a table.

Señor Santiago and Javier, hobbling on crutches, immediately went over to the astonished guests. Señor Santiago began, "Padre Reynolds, I wanted to show my appreciation for your special ministry in preparing young men for the priesthood and for coming to Mexico and bringing Nicholas and Jose with you.

"Mother Monica and all the Sisters also wanted to thank you for your spiritual guidance and Masses for them and for their boys. And all the boys here wanted to thank Nicholas and Jose for helping them with their English, and for their time and effort in coaching them in soccer and helping them become good enough to play against other schools.

"But most of all, I wanted to thank Nicholas and Jose for their spiritual comfort and courageous effort that helped save the life of my son, Javier, and the life of Pablo. Because of their faith and love of Our Lord, they have made me realize that their calling to be a priest is truly a great gift for our Catholic Church. They also have made me realize that it is not power, money or material things that are important. It is doing the Will of God that is important and that brings one peace and joy. So, this celebration is a thank-you from all of us."

Mother Monica stepped in and said, "Yes, and everyone here at Holy Family wants to thank you, too, Señor Santiago for everything that you have done for us. Because of you, every boy who leaves Holy Family will now have the opportunity to work in your factory. And how can we ever thank you for paying for a soccer coach so that my boys will be able to play soccer games against the other schools in San Miguel de Allende. Now before we enjoy the wonderful food that Señor Santiago has provided us with, Father Reynolds would you say a prayer."

"Dear God, we pray in gratitude for this meal and your many blessings. Please continue to guide and protect us through the intercession of Our Lady of Guadalupe, Saint Jose Sanchez del Rio and all the angels and saints. We ask all of this through Christ, Our Lord. Amen."

When the prayer had ended, Jose and Nicholas each gave Javier a hug, being careful not to knock him over.

"Well, I see that you finally aren't attached to your bed anymore," joked Jose.

"Yes," Nicholas added. "The last time we saw you was when your dad took us to your home when you got out of the hospital."

"Before you go home, I had to tell the both of you how blessed I am to have you as my friends and to thank you for saving my life," responded Javier.

It was Jose who spoke up, "We only did what you would have done if we were the ones with a broken leg."

Señor Santiago said in a serious voice, "There is something that I must share with you, Padre Reynolds, and with Nicholas and Jose.

"When I was notified that Javier was missing after the earthquake, even though I was greatly upset, I didn't turn to God for help. I was told that the search and rescue teams would have to wait until daylight. That night I had a hard time sleeping.

"When I did fall asleep, I had this dream. I saw Saint Jose Sanchez del Rio and he was standing on a hill with a big cross in the background. He was waving the flag of the Cristeros with the image of Our Lady of Guadalupe on it. And all around him were hundreds of young people and they were all shouting, *'Viva Christo Rey!'* And among the young people I saw Javier, Nicholas and Jose. Then I woke up.

"It was so real that I immediately prayed to Saint Jose asking him for his help to bring my son back to me alive. I told him that I didn't have his courage to die for Christ, but I did have the courage to see how I was hurting my son by not letting him do the Will of God. And I told Saint Jose that I would let Javier follow his calling to be a Catholic priest."

With a big smile on his face, Javier said, "In the fall I will be going to college at the Pontifical University of Mexico where I will be majoring in Theology. I know that I have been greatly blessed with both of my parents now praying for my vocation."

If it wasn't for Father Reynolds supporting Javier, he would have fallen over with the big hugs that both Nicholas and Jose gave him again.

"Oh, Javier, this is wonderful news. This means that we can go to your ordination, and when we are ordained priests two years later, you can come to ours," Jose exclaimed.

Nicholas, looking intently at Javier, said, "Remember when we went to Saint James Church and you asked me if you could be what God wanted you to be and not what your father wanted. When we prayed a Rosary in front of the shrine of Saint Jose, I prayed for you and I asked Our Lady to help change the heart of your father so that you could follow your calling to be a Catholic priest. And like Father Kelly would say, *'do not underestimate the power given to the great Mother of God.'* Now if you will excuse me, there is someone I have to see before I leave Mexico."

Nicholas then walked over to Pablo and, sitting down next to him, said, "Pablo, I needed to see you before I go back home."

"Yes, amigo, I also needed to see you because there is so much I want to tell you. When you left me to find help, I kept praying on your rosary beads to Our Lady of Guadalupe to protect the life of you, Jose and Javier. Our Lady brought me great comfort and because you baptized me, I knew I was saved from my sins and I was not afraid to die.

"When they found me, I guess I was pretty bad. I don't remember anything until I woke up in the hospital. I was still groggy and felt not good. I tried to see if the doctors had taken care of the snake's bite and that is when I realized that my leg was gone. But then I saw Padre Reynolds and you next to my bed, and I knew I would be okay."

With sadness in his eyes and in a voice full of compassion, Nicholas replied, "Oh Pablo, I was so thankful to God that you did not die. But at the same time, I felt such guilt and such great sadness. You saved me from that rattlesnake, and because it bit you instead of me your leg had to be amputated."

"Oh, Amigo, don't feel guilty or sad. The doctors told me that the snake's poison damaged my flesh so much and that is why they had to take my leg. And they told me that it was a miracle that the snake's poison didn't kill me.

"And then you told me about your miracle with Our Lady of Guadalupe and your angel, Raphael, and I knew that God was watching over us in a big way. Besides, God is very good to me. Senor Santiago is going to arrange for me to have an artificial leg. Now I won't be a burden, for I still have many things I have to do for the Sisters and the boys here."

"Oh, Pablo, that's wonderful and I know that you will be able to do everything you did before to help the Sisters."

In a gentle voice, Pablo continued, "Nicholas, there was a reason why you came to Mexico. Our Lady of Guadalupe would never have changed my heart if I didn't take you to her shrine. But there is something more. You see, because you took Miguel with you during Christmas to the home of the Santiagos, Javier's mama and papa saw the special friendship that Javier and Miguel have. Now they are going to bring him into their home and make him part of their family."

"Oh Pablo, I am so happy for Miguel. The Santiagos are a wonderful family and now Miguel will not only have a brother, he will have three sisters."

"See, amigo, you have done much good and you have changed so many lives here, including a sinner like me. Priests are very special and you are very special. Some day when you are a priest, you will do even greater good and change the lives of many sinners like me. Nicholas, you will always be *mi querido amigo* and every day of my life, I will pray for you."

Nicholas, who always was very emotional, put his arms around Pablo, then he buried his head in Pablo's strong shoulder and quietly said, "Pablo, you will always be *my dear friend* and every day of my life, I will pray for you."

About the Authors

Father Stephen Gemme and Deacon George O'Connor are co-authors of the Nicholas Gilroy books. Nicholas Gilroy–Viva Christo Rey is the second book in the series. Nicholas Gilroy–Our Lady and the Guardian is the first book in the series. Both books are available on Amazon.

Both authors have taught in Catholic schools. Father Stephen taught history and social studies to students in high school. He is the Chaplain at Saint Vincent Hospital in Worcester, MA. Deacon George taught math, science and religion to students in sixth, seventh and eighth grades, and he is a parish deacon.

Contact them at nicholasgilroy2017@gmail.com or follow them on Facebook: Nicholas Gilroy Our Lady and the Guardian.

The Nicholas Gilroy books are the inspiration of the Blessed Virgin Mary.